TEN 10-MINUTE PLAYS

VOLUME I

Edited by

WALTER WYKES

Black Box Press
Los Angeles

ISBN 978-1-4303-0022-9

First Edition

CONTENTS

THE SALMON TRIBUNAL

WALTER WYKES

The Salmon Tribunal premiered at Cafe Copioh in Las Vegas, Nevada on August 30, 1997, under the direction of Greg Vovos. The cast was as follows:

JUNE: Maggie Winn-Jones
NORMA: Michelle Caudel

SETTING:
A restaurant.

*[The Fisherman's Wharf—an upscale restaurant in the
middle of a busy, downtown metropolitan area. JUNE sits at
a small table, glancing vaguely at her menu. She is an older
woman—well-groomed and elegantly dressed. She checks her
watch periodically, looks about, and then returns to the menu.
Finally, NORMA enters and joins JUNE at the table. NORMA
does not have JUNE's sense of style, but she is younger and
more attractive. JUNE ignores her, takes a sip of wine, and
continues to peruse the menu.]*

NORMA: All right, I'm here.
　　[Pause.]
I'm here.
　　[Pause.]
I don't know why I've come, but I have. I've flown here. Dropped
everything and come running. Not out of fear, mind you. Not in the
least. I want to make that clear. I'm not afraid of you. In fact, that's
why I've come. To make it clear. Now ... what is it you have to say?
　　[Pause.]
I've just asked you a question.
　　[Pause.]
Are you going to sit there and ignore me now that I've driven all the
way out here? Now that I've dropped everything and stood up to you.
Have you lost your nerve? Is that it?

JUNE: Would you recommend the salmon?

NORMA: What's that?

JUNE: The salmon. I'm not familiar with the salmon. I thought you
might help me out.

NORMA: Help you out?

JUNE: That's right. I'm partial to salmon, but only if it's prepared
just so. I'm sure you understand. Bad salmon, it's difficult to
stomach.

NORMA: I don't go in for salmon.

JUNE: Well, even so, you might offer some general insight into the care with which this particular establishment prepares its food. You have eaten here before ... haven't you?
>   *[Pause.]*

NORMA: Yes.

JUNE: I thought you might have. It's such a convenient spot. For a quick lunch perhaps.
>   *[Pause.]*
And you've never tried the salmon?

NORMA: No.

JUNE: That's a shame. It's really very good. I have tried it, actually, I've only just remembered. Several times, in fact. I enjoyed it very much. That's what I'll have. The salmon.

NORMA: You didn't call me here to talk about fish.

JUNE: Fish? No ... no, I suppose not.

NORMA: No.

JUNE: Not exactly. Although Murray does like his fish. He still goes in for fish now and then, doesn't he? Salmon, in fact, if I remember correctly. I'm surprised you haven't had a bite. Perhaps you have, and you've forgotten.
>   *[Pause.]*

NORMA: He tells me you've taken to calling the office.

JUNE: Has he?

NORMA: Yes. He has.

JUNE: Well, he was probably worried you'd find out from one of the girls. Cynthia perhaps. I always liked Cynthia. I found her very pleasant. Don't you?

NORMA: Cynthia and I are very close.

JUNE: Yes, I adored her. We used to get along quite well, Cynthia and I. We'd even meet for lunch now and then. Although she never warned me. Never a word, you understand. Only that guilty silence. There's no question where her true loyalty lies.
   [Pause.]
Have you ever noticed ... Murray has quite a talent for masking his indiscretions behind little bits of truth. Don't you think? I'm sure you remember. I mean, I'm sure you were party to it in the past. He's quite conscious of it, I know. In fact, he's probably bragged about it from time to time. Take, for instance, my calling the office. Now ... why tell you? What might motivate him to keep you informed? He certainly knows it won't please you. Why not keep it to himself? Hmmm? Well ... let's think about that for a moment. Perhaps my calls are an annoyance, and he wants you to be aware of them, you know, as a measure of his honesty—as proof that he has nothing to hide. How does that sound? He wouldn't tell you about my calls, for instance, if we'd taken to seeing each other on occasion for a quick lunch, now would he?
   [Pause.]
 Would he?
   [Pause.]
A quick poke in the afternoon? Don't you think he'd keep the evidence to himself?
   [Pause.]
I don't know if salmon sounds quite right after all. Perhaps just a salad. At my age, you know, one has to pay a little more attention if one wants to maintain one's girlish figure.

NORMA: What exactly are you trying to say?

JUNE: I'm not saying anything. I'm only talking. It's conversation. I'm sure you'd notice if there was something, you know, going on. An affair, if that's what you want to call it. After all, you've been on the other side. You know what it's like. You wouldn't be fooled as easily as I was.

NORMA: No.

JUNE: No. Certainly not. Would you like some wine? A dry white wine to go with your salmon? I assume you'll want salmon. That's what I'm having.

NORMA: I don't drink.

JUNE: No?

NORMA: Not at the moment.

JUNE: How unfortunate. A few glasses of wine, and I'm sure we could have shared some interesting stories, you and I.

NORMA: I have certain ... considerations.
      [Pause.]

JUNE: Considerations?

NORMA: That's right.
      [JUNE laughs.]

JUNE: You know, I ... I almost feel sorry for you. Almost.
      [Pause.]
Does Murray know?
      [Pause.]
I know he always *professed* to want a family, but, you know, to be perfectly honest, I never quite believed him. I mean, he's a bit too selfish for fatherhood, don't you think? Personally, I was always afraid his attentions would waver once the pounds started to pile on, you know, he'd start spending more and more evenings at the office

where he could pound out his frustrations on that big oak desk of his. Did you ever do it on that big oak desk?

NORMA: Stay away from him.

JUNE: What's that?

NORMA: Stay away from my husband.

JUNE: There! You've said it! Now it's all out in the open! All laid out, nice and easy!

NORMA: I'll have the secretaries instructed not to put you through.

JUNE: Don't you feel a bit hypocritical? Just a twinge? I can't help it if he needs a good poke in the afternoon. I'm only accommodating him, really. I don't go out of my way anymore. I don't have to. Not that I wouldn't—don't get me wrong. I have certain "considerations" of my own. Not that kind! Don't be ridiculous! At my age? No ... no, it's much more ... urgent, really.
 [Pause.]
I've contemplated making contact with Murray for some time. I suspected he might be receptive to the idea. After all, it worked against me—why not the other way around? But I just didn't have the impetus until now, you know? I needed a little push. And there's nothing like a deadline to get the old blood flowing. All the juices, really. It doesn't follow, if you think about it. You'd assume certain things ... certain activities ... would become unimportant. Certain betrayals would become unbearable. But they don't really. In fact, quite the opposite. Everything takes on a new light. The impossible becomes possible, desirable even. It's quite remarkable. That's what I called for, really. To let you know. I thought it might expedite matters.
 [Pause.]
I have nothing to lose and little time to do it. The salmon swimming upstream, you know.

NORMA: He left for a reason.

JUNE: Yes. He was lured away.

NORMA: No.

JUNE: You played to his weakness. I can do the same.

NORMA: It's not a game.

JUNE: Oh, but it is! It is a game! Cat and mouse! Only I didn't know it before! You had an unfair advantage! By the time I knew the game was being played, we were already in the thick of it! You'd already won! Not this time. It won't be so easy this time around!

NORMA: He left for a reason. He'll remember that.

JUNE: Oh, honey ... they always leave for a reason.

NORMA: You'll remind him one way or another.
        [Pause. NORMA rises.]

JUNE: I suppose I should be going as well. I have an appointment later this afternoon, and I don't want to be late. Do you want to tip the waiter or should I? You know what, don't worry about it. I'll just put it on my card. Oh, one question. Will you tell him we met today?
        [Pause.]

NORMA: Will you?
        [Silence.]

* * *

THE DMV ONE

NICK ZAGONE

The DMV One was first professionally produced at the Iron Ring Theatre Company in Turlock, California on April 28, 2006, under the direction of Gary Bowman. The cast was as follows:

MAN: Mark Hansen
WOMAN: Carin Heidelbach
OTHER WOMAN: Danelle Dupré

SETTING:
DMV office.

[At lights up a MAN stands waiting for a WOMAN sitting at her desk. The Woman is crying while typing on her computer. She then sees the Man. He waves. She cleans up and takes the "CLOSED" sign off her desk.]

WOMAN: Can I help you?

MAN: Yes you can! I just moved here from out of state and I need a new driver's license and registration.

WOMAN: All right. Any tickets in the last four years?

MAN: No…

WOMAN: Any arrests?

MAN: Nope.

WOMAN: Warrants?

MAN: No.

WOMAN: Convictions?

MAN: No.

WOMAN: Single?

MAN: What?

WOMAN: Marital status. Single?

MAN: Yes, how'd you…?

WOMAN: No ring. Divorced or Gay?

MAN: What?

WOMAN: It's a new Gallup survey. Divorced or Gay?

MAN: Gallup survey...? I don't see what...

WOMAN: Divorced or Gay!

MAN: Neither! Single! Never been married! Hetero!

WOMAN: Past relationships?

MAN: I don't see what this has to do with...?

WOMAN: Only take a moment. Any past long-term intimate relationships please?

MAN: Like heavy duty?
    [WOMAN nods.]
Well of course...

WOMAN: How many? One. Two. Or more than one or two?

MAN: Well... one.

WOMAN: How long? Less than one year? More than one year? Or "Not really over yet because every so often you still get drunk and make 'booty calls?'"

MAN: Does it say that?

WOMAN: Please just answer the question.

MAN: Four years. And it's over.

WOMAN: *(after a pause)* Live together?

MAN: It doesn't say that!

WOMAN: It says "dated," "lived together" or... "Other."

MAN: Fine. I don't know what "other" is, so I guess we lived together.

WOMAN: *(under her breath)* Free milk from the cow...

MAN: What was that?

WOMAN: Nothing.

MAN: Listen. I just want to get my driver's license and registration okay?

WOMAN: Did you love her?

MAN: She didn't want to get married okay!?

WOMAN: *(typing this in)* "Loved her but says it is over." All right. I need your current driver's license, current registration, old license plates and tags, smog inspection certificate, VIN tags and verification, proof of insurance from an in-state provider, social security number, driving record, the blue book on your car, and a letter from your mommy.
> *[MAN has frantically produced all the WOMAN requires, making a pile of papers on her desk.]*

MAN: Ha! Got it all! Right here!

WOMAN: *(picking through the pile, she spots something)* This registration expired yesterday.

MAN: I know...

WOMAN: Have you driven your car since yesterday?

MAN: No.

WOMAN: No!? How did you get here then?

MAN: *(points off)* Her.

WOMAN: Who's that? Your new girlfriend? That bitch!

MAN: That's my sister.

WOMAN: Oh. Can she verify that in a court of law?!

MAN: Can we get on with this please?

WOMAN: All right. *(facing her computer terminal and typing)* Car or truck?

MAN: Car.

WOMAN: Two wheel or four?

MAN: Two.

WOMAN: V-6 or V-8?

MAN: V-8.

WOMAN: Hmmmm. Camero or Mustang?

MAN: Mustang.

WOMAN: HMmmmm! Income per year. 10 grand to 20? 20 to 30? 30 to 40? 50 plus?

MAN: The DMV wants to know my income?

WOMAN: And that's Net, not Gross.

MAN: Well if all goes well, 50 plus.

WOMAN: Boxers or Briefs?

MAN: What?

WOMAN: Boxers or Briefs.
    *[MAN realizes what's going on, and decides to play the
    game.]*

MAN: All right. Okay. Boxers or Briefs. Right now?

WOMAN: Yes.

MAN: Boxers.

WOMAN: Person type: A or B?

MAN: A.

WOMAN: Person type: Night or Morning?

MAN: Night.

WOMAN: We exchange numbers or you ask me out right now?

MAN: Right now.

WOMAN: Drinks or Dinner?

MAN: Dinner.

WOMAN: French or Italian?

MAN: French.

WOMAN: Wine or beer?

MAN: Wine.

WOMAN: Cash or Credit?

MAN: Cash.

WOMAN: Your place or mine?

MAN: Mine.
  [They become a bit excited, breathing heavy, this builds...]

WOMAN: Wells or Hitchcock?

MAN: Hitchcock.

WOMAN: Salinger or Kerouac?

MAN: Kerouac.

WOMAN: Lennon or McCartney?!

MAN: Lennon! Bra clasp front or back?

WOMAN: None!

MAN: Oh my god!

WOMAN: Slow or fast?

MAN: Fast!

WOMAN: Heels on or off?

MAN: For God's sake on! Wait! Condom or...

WOMAN: Pill!

MAN: Yes!

WOMAN: Top or bottom?!

MAN: Top!

WOMAN: Over or under?!

MAN: Who cares!?

WOMAN: Want or need?! Buy or sell?! Tie me up or tie me down?! Bob or Carol or Ted or Alice?!

MAN: Parsley!

WOMAN: Sage!

MAN: Rosemary!

WOMAN: Thyme!

MAN: YES or NO!

WOMAN: Ginger or Mary Ann?!

MAN: MRS. BRADY!
        [WOMAN finally orgasms big time.]

WOMAN: Yes! Oh my God!!!
        [BOTH are breathing heavy. A beat.]
Smoke or clove?

MAN: Smoke.
        [They smoke. Another beat.]

WOMAN: Out to a movie or rent?

MAN: Rent.

WOMAN: Meet my friends or yours.

MAN: Mine.

WOMAN: We argue or fight.

MAN: Fight.

WOMAN: You make up with flowers, or roses?

MAN: Roses.

WOMAN: Big wedding or small?

MAN: Big.

WOMAN: House or apartment?

MAN: House.

WOMAN: Carpet or Hardwood.

MAN: Carpet.

WOMAN: One kid or two?

MAN: One.

WOMAN: Christmas at my parents or yours?

MAN: Mine.

WOMAN: Stay up with me and talk? Or got to… sleep?
     [MAN is already snoring.]

WOMAN: *[putting out her cigarette]* All right, just a few more questions… before I give you your… license and registration. Are you asleep? I said are you sleeping?!
     [MAN wakes with a start.]

MAN: No! No. *(after a beat)* Do I get my license and registration now?

WOMAN: Well that's what I wanted to talk to you about.

MAN: What? I gave you everything I was supposed to have, I met all the requirements!

WOMAN: You just don't get it do you?!

MAN: *(showing her the papers)* I have done everything I can to make you happy!

WOMAN: All this?! *(taking papers and throwing them at him)* All this means nothing to me!

MAN: You got problems. I'm going to your manager. Maybe she'll give me my license and registration! Maybe your manager will give me what I NEED!!

WOMAN: No! Don't!

MAN: What is your problem!

WOMAN: *(turning back to her terminal, typing on her keyboard)* Oh look, says here you have a suspended license how bout that?

MAN: What are you doing?

WOMAN: And look here, a warrant for your arrest!

MAN: Wait!

WOMAN: You seem to be on the FBI's Ten Most Wanted List, of all the crazy things!

MAN: Stop! Stop! Stop it! Look, I'm sorry. I want to go back. Before. To the way we were, remember? You would ask me questions. And I would answer? It was so wonderful. I want that feeling back. How 'bout it? You and me? Can you feel it in your heart to try again? Give me one more chance?

WOMAN: *(through her tears)* I'm sorry. It's too late. Too late for that.

MAN: No. Please no...

WOMAN: Here are your new plates, your tags, your license and this...

MAN: Is it... my registration?

WOMAN: *(nodding)* Your walkin' papers. This hurts me as much as it hurts you.

MAN: *(signing registration)* You don't know that. I don't even think I can go on.

WOMAN: You'll be back. Next year, and the year after, and the year after that—

MAN: I have no regrets.

WOMAN: As long as men and women need cars, people like us will go on loving each other.

MAN: Good-bye.
   [He exits. She's crying. A beat. ANOTHER WOMAN enters and stands waiting.]

WOMAN: *(getting herself together)* Can I help you?

ANOTHER WOMAN: Yes you can. I moved here from out of state and I need a new license and registration.

WOMAN: Any tickets in the last four years?

ANOTHER WOMAN: No.

WOMAN: Any arrests?

ANOTHER WOMAN: No.

WOMAN: Warrants?

ANOTHER WOMAN: No.

WOMAN: Convictions?

ANOTHER WOMAN: No.
  [A beat. WOMAN smiles, then takes a deep breath.]

WOMAN: Married or single?

BLACKOUT

GRAY MATTER

JEANETTE D. FARR

Gray Matter premiered at the University of Nevada, Las Vegas, on March 4, 1998, under the direction of Mutsuko Nakamura. The cast was as follows:

MARGE: Nancy Frederick
RUSSELL: Derick Swinson

CHARACTERS:
MARGE: 66 years old. Well-dressed, middle-class, white woman.
RUSSELL: 21 years old. African-American male. Wears baggy clothes and a baseball cap.

SETTING:
Small room in a police station. It somewhat resembles a doctor's waiting room, but not as comfortable. There is a row of 6 chairs and a counter. On the counter is a clipboard with a pencil attached with string and a "front desk" bell. Behind the counter is a computer generated sign that reads: "PLEASE SIGN IN".

[MARGE is sitting in a middle seat in the row of chairs. She is reading, doing a crossword puzzle, knitting - something to occupy her time. SHE has her purse on the seat next to her. RUSSELL enters, looks around notices sign, signs in, then moves to find a seat. MARGE, not looking up, moves her purse to the other side of her and tucks it close.]

RUSSELL: I saw that.

MARGE: Excuse me?

RUSSELL: I caught you.

MARGE: I don't know you.

RUSSELL: When I walked in, you moved your bag.

MARGE: Please. I don't want any trouble.

RUSSELL: I'm not—

MARGE: Because if you're causing trouble, I can notify someone.

RUSSELL: I wasn't—

MARGE: OK then.
        (PAUSE)

RUSSELL: Do I make you nervous?

MARGE: I don't even know you.

RUSSELL: Doesn't matter. I can still make you nervous.

MARGE: Look, I was in the middle of something, if you don't mind.

RUSSELL: Why did you move your bag?

MARGE: I was getting some gum.

29

[SHE searches for a piece of gum.]

RUSSELL: Can I have a piece?

MARGE: It's Juicy Fruit.

RUSSELL: My favorite.

MARGE: I only have a stick.

RUSSELL: Can I have half?

MARGE: You're bothering me.

RUSSELL: Ok. So I don't make you nervous, but I bother you?

MARGE: I'm just not in the mood for... conversation.

RUSSELL: I think it's something else.

MARGE: If you say so.
       [MARGE goes back to her "project."]

RUSSELL: When I walked through that door you thought: Rapist, murderer, purse-stealer.

MARGE: I thought no such thing.

RUSSELL: But you moved your purse.

MARGE: I was just being polite by making more room. I would do that for anyone.

RUSSELL: I don't buy it.

MARGE: It doesn't really concern me if you buy it or not. That's the reason.

RUSSELL: There are five empty chairs I could sit in.

MARGE: All right. *(As if to satisfy him)* You caught me.

RUSSELL: Unless you wanted me to come sit next to you.

MARGE: You sit where you'd like.
  [RUSSELL sits in the chair farthest away from her.]

RUSSELL: This one's too hard.
  [HE moves to the third chair closest to her.]

RUSSELL: Nope. Not right either.
  [HE gets two chairs away.]

RUSSELL: Damn uncomfortable!
  [HE sits next to her.]

RUSSELL: Do you mind if I try yours? This one isn't right either.
How 'bout you let me sit on your lap.
  [MARGE goes to counter and rings the bell.]

RUSSELL: Wait, wait, lady! I was only joking. Sit back down!

MARGE: Will you leave me alone?

RUSSELL: I'll be nice. I'll even sit over here if it'll make you happy.
  [MARGE sits far away from RUSSELL.]

RUSSELL: Why are you here?

MARGE: Why are YOU here?

RUSSELL: I came to see my parole officer.

MARGE: Nice.

RUSSELL: Does that bother you?

MARGE: And you wondered why I moved my purse.

RUSSELL: But when I walked in you didn't know I was coming to see my parole officer. You just saw me and assumed I was a criminal.

MARGE: I followed my instincts. When the fight or flight kicks in you should listen to that. What you just said about you being a criminal was exactly what my gut was telling me.

RUSSELL: So you moved your purse.

MARGE: Right.

RUSSELL: Wow. You knew. I guess I can't go anywhere anymore. That must be why people cross the street when they see me comin'. It's just like B.O. Nobody ever tells you that you have B.O. until it's too late. Then you come home after realizing you forgot to put on deodorant and wonder why in the hell nobody has been talking to you. Thank you. Thank you for letting me know you can actually see or FEEL through your instinctual animal feelings that there is criminal written all over my face.

MARGE: I'm sure if you dressed a little better, that might help too.

RUSSELL: Maybe kick down a few bucks, get a nice suit or something....

MARGE: Clean yourself up a little.

RUSSELL: Sure. Thanks. You've really helped me uh... What's your name?

MARGE: Why do you want to know my name?

RUSSELL: Well, I can't tell all my "convict" friends that some nice lady helped me. I'd like to tie a name to a face.

MARGE: I don't think you need to know my name.

RUSSELL: Come on.

MARGE: If I tell you, you'll.... leave me alone?

RUSSELL: Cross my heart!

MARGE: Sheila.

RUSSELL: What?

MARGE: That's my name. Sheila.

RUSSELL: Ok. *(PAUSE)* It's a sin to lie.

MARGE: I know that.

RUSSELL: You feel ok being a liar.

MARGE: Who said I was lying?

RUSSELL: You don't look like a Sheila. Sheila is a young beautiful lady's name.

MARGE: Thank you.

RUSSELL: No, no, no—don't take this wrong. But you ain't a Sheila.

MARGE: You get a name at birth and you keep a name for life. Even beautiful young women named Sheila eventually grow older.

RUSSELL: Yeah, but they don't grow up to look like you.

MARGE: How can you tell what a person should be called or not.

RUSSELL: You said I looked like a criminal.

MARGE: I did not.

RUSSELL: Did you or did you not just admit to me that I looked like a criminal. That you had a gut instinct—and you were right, weren't you?

MARGE: Let's just let it go, ok?

RUSSELL: Sheila?
     [SHE doesn't respond.]
Hey, Sheila. That is your name isn't it?

MARGE: Yes.

RUSSELL: For a minute there, I thought you didn't know.

 MARGE: What is it.

RUSSELL: I wasn't exactly truthful with you a minute ago.

MARGE: Really.

RUSSELL: I'm not here to see my parole officer.

MARGE: That's nice.

RUSSELL: I don't even have a police record.

MARGE: Fine.

RUSSELL: Yet I look like a criminal.

MARGE: Well, what else was I supposed to think-

RUSSELL: Why?

MARGE: Why what?

RUSSELL: Why did you assume that I was a criminal? Was it because of this?

[HE points to the palm of his hand.]

MARGE: Your hand?

RUSSELL: No. Closer. Look. Right here. See it?
[MARGE moves closer to his hand, she is curious. Just as she gets close enough he forms his hand into a fist.]

MARGE: I don't see anything.

RUSSELL: Simple as that. *(HE points to his fist)* Black. *(HE points to her face)* and white.
[There is a long pause. Just as MARGE is about to speak, RUSSELL goes over to the counter, leans over, and looks around.]

MARGE: I haven't seen anyone at that counter in a while. They told me to wait.

RUSSELL: Man. This is messed up. Always like the government. Keep you waiting as long as they want to. Unless of course you've done something wrong, then they're up your ass with a microscope. I can't be waiting all day. *(Ringing the bell)* Hey! Anyone there?

MARGE: The best thing is probably to just sit quietly and wait.

RUSSELL: I'm here on my lunch hour, man! *(To himself)* I can't come back to work late, they'll have my ass.

MARGE: Where do you work?

RUSSELL: Excuse me?

MARGE: Your job. Where do you have to go?

RUSSELL: I get it. *(Pause)* I have a job, so it's ok to talk to me, now.

MARGE: I just wondered how far you had to walk.

RUSSELL: I drove myself down here. Jesus, lady! We LIBERALS have cars too, you know. Maybe not nice ones like you folks but at least it gets me from point A to point B, and I bought it with hard earned workin' man's money.

MARGE: I didn't mean—

RUSSELL: You didn't mean. Don't tell me you didn't mean. I may be what at least 45 years younger than you but I'm not stupid! I know what you meant.

MARGE: Please. Don't be so sensitive, I—

RUSSELL: What. Am I wrong? Did I jump to conclusions about what you just said? Am I misunderstanding you?

MARGE: Yes!

RUSSELL: *(Calm, direct, and to the point)* Now you know how it feels.

MARGE: I don't know what you are trying to prove here.

RUSSELL: I assumed things about you just like you assumed things about me when I walked through that door. I'm not trying to change the way you think, I'm just telling you how it goes. You can't tell me that if an elderly white woman was sitting next to you instead of me that you wouldn't be exchanging recipes and complaining about your arthritis or whatever the hell you all do. You certainly wouldn't have jumped out of your skin like you did when I walked in here.

MARGE: Would it make you happy if I gave you my recipe for pot roast?

RUSSELL: Aw, man!

MARGE: I won't give anyone that recipe you know. Not even my sister. The key is the marinade.

RUSSELL: Forget it.

MARGE: You say "that's what we do" so I'm following through with it.

RUSSELL: I'm just saying you wouldn't be so uptight if I was someone different.

MARGE: Uptight! The reason I'm uptight has nothing to do with who you are.

RUSSELL: Don't bother apologizing for who YOU are. You don't have to talk to me or trust that I'm not going to take something of yours. If that's what you believe—then—way it goes.

MARGE: I don't trust anyone at the moment! *(Pause, having trouble getting this out)* Somewhere between here and Thirteenth Street I've misplaced my wallet. The sad thing about it is it had a lot of money in it not to mention my driver's license and pictures of my grandchildren. I don't even care about the money, but the fact that someone out there knows my identity isn't too comforting to me. I came down here to file a report in hopes that someone would be honest enough to... What was I thinking? I've wasted half my day in here just for one chance that there is one honest person left in this world.

RUSSELL: I'm sorry. I'm sure someone will find it.

MARGE: Oh, I'm sure someone has found it by now and had a tine time maxing my gold card. I don't know why I'm wasting my time.
    [MARGE gets up to leave.]

RUSSELL: Hey, Sheila. Why don't you wait a few more minutes. I'm sure if we make enough noise, someone will come out to help us.
    [MARGE stops.]

MARGE: May I tell you something?

RUSSELL: Sure. *(Pause)* What is it?

MARGE: You did catch me.

RUSSELL: No sweat... I mean, I didn't know.

MARGE: My name... it isn't Sheila.

RUSSELL: Well whadaya know? Really? 'Cause I was convinced that...

MARGE: Don't be funny. Actually it's...

RUSSELL: Marge.

MARGE: What—How?

RUSSELL: You just LOOK like a Marge to me.

MARGE: *(Amazed)* You're good at that.

RUSSELL: And ... It says it on your license.
    [HE reaches into his pocket and pulls out a ladies' wallet.]

RUSSELL: Here.

MARGE: You—Where?

RUSSELL: I tried phoning, but there was no answer.
    [MARGE opens up her wallet.]

RUSSELL: You can count it if you want. I didn't take nothin'.

MARGE: Come here.

RUSSELL: Aw, lady. I didn't take any of it! I just found it like that—
    [MARGE takes out a photo and shows it to RUSSELL.]

MARGE: This is my granddaughter. THIS is Sheila.

RUSSELL: *(Smiling.)* She's pretty. I can see the resemblance.

MARGE: *(A beat—SHE stands)* Well, no use staying around here if I don't have to and YOU need to get yourself back to work. You'd better cross your name off that list. Don't want some government employee working too hard calling your name.

RUSSELL: They have to do something.
> *[MARGE exits without her purse which she left on the chair. RUSSELL goes over to clipboard and crosses out his name. HE turns around, runs over to the purse and picks it up.]*

RUSSELL: Hey, Marge, you forgot your—

MARGE: I forgot my—

RUSSELL & MARGE: *(Simultaneously)* Purse.

MARGE: *(Taking her bag.)* Thank you.

LIGHTS FADE

JOLLY JACK JUNIOR
The Buccaneer's Bairn

JEFF GOODE

Jolly Jack Junior: The Buccaneer's Bairn premiered on August 17, 2005, at the Nexus Theatre in Perth, Australia, under the direction of Amy Tyers. The cast was as follows:

WILLY: Stuart McLay
WENCH: Amy Tyers

SETTING:
The Deck of a Sailing Ship.

[The Deck of a Sailing Ship – "The Boatswain's Booty"]

[Sounds of a sea battle raging – cannonfire and sabers clashing - pirates boarding the ship. PIRATE WILLY bounds onto the stage, a cutlass in either hand.]

WILLY: Avast, ye brigands! Yo ho! Strike colors and submit to be boarded. *(calling to his crew:)* Haul aft to the helm, me hearties. Hoist the mizzenpoop and trim fast the doozy. Take no prisoners, save the women and agile boys. And a lubbard's blarney to the bloke who brings me the brigands' captain. Harrr![1]

WENCH: *(offstage:)* Unhand me, ye scurvy scuttlefish!

WILLY: Man that woman, mate, she's gettin' away! Mind your starboard jowl! No, yer starboard!
　　　[A resounding SMACK from offstage. WILLY winces. A PIRATE WENCH rushes in and tries to get past him, but he sheathes his blade and catches her in one arm.]
Hold there, sea wench! Where ye think yer garn?

WENCH: To hell's britches ere I answer to the likes of you, ye daft cutlet. This be a pirate vessel, ye've boarded. We're all pirates here!

WILLY: Aye, and it's pirates I'm pillaging today - the devil take 'em – for I am one-eyed Willy, the buccaneer's bane. Have ye not heard o' me?

WENCH: Nay, I think I'd remember that.

WILLY: Well, I'm new. *(then with gusto:)* Orphaned by pirates I was! And I mean to have me revenge on every last scoundrel. Now take me to your captain 'fore I do something I might not regret.

WENCH: What, will you have your pleasures with me unwilling corpse, you filthy, whoreson, motherless son of a sea cow?

---

[1] Author's Note: Some of these words are made up.

43

WILLY: Motherless I be—for orphaned by pirates I was—but I'd sooner suckle a manatee's teat than mingle my bilges with the likes of you, ya withered old crone. Why, you must be nearly 28, by the looks of ye.

WENCH: I don't look a day over 25, an' you know it, ye scurrilous scallywag. And I may be withered – by contemporary standards – but I'm still as fine a piece of sea bass as you'll never lay fingers on. Now unfist me before I pluck out your other eye, ye couthless bootblack.

WILLY: Nay, and ye'll nae touch me good eye, till I've seen your captain with it. Now where be the brigand?

WENCH: What would the likes of you want with the likes of Captain Jack?

WILLY: Captain Jack? Did you say, Captain Jack??

WENCH: Aye, Captain Jack, the terror and scourge of the high seas, and some of the low ones, too. What's the matter, mate? Ye look weak in the gills at the very sound of the name. And rightly so, for there's no more treacherous pirate on land or sea. Or up in space, for that matter. Ye've good reason to be terrified.

WILLY: Terrified? I don't know the meaning of the word!

WENCH: It means scared.

WILLY: I know what it means! I was being facetious.

WENCH: I don't know the meaning of the word!
        [He rolls his eye at her, but goes on.]

WILLY: Fear is for cowards, says I. And I'll have none of it!

WENCH: Then why do ye tremble in yer galoshes at the mere mention of Captain Jack? *(He flinches at the mention. So she does it again.)* Cap'n Jack! Cap'n Jack!

WILLY: Shut your fish hole, ye briny deck trollop! I'm not afeared o' your Captain Jack.

WENCH: Ha! So yer a coward and a liar, to boot!

WILLY: Nae, but I tell ye true, sea slut, it pangs me to hear the name, because I've sought this Captain Jack for near me entire life. Since I was naught but a wee bairn in me swaddles growin' up in a lubbard's orphanage north of New Norfolk, I prayed myself to sleep at night cursing the name of Cap'n Jack, the pirate that orphaned me. I'd lie abed awake in that unholy monastery with nothing but me simmering hatred and the love o' God to feed me when the cruel nuns would not. No sooner was I old enough to be out of me diapers, than I set off in quest of me quarry. I searched the world over, far and wide, o'er hill and mountain, desert and near-desert. And then I figured out Captain Jack was a pirate name, and I started searching the seas.

WENCH: You poor wastling. And how long have you been questing?

WILLY: Nigh on three weeks.

WENCH: Three weeks without diapers?! How do you bear it?

WILLY: Double thick breeches, lass. Double thick breeches.

WENCH: But what's so all-bloody important about catchin' Captain Jack?

WILLY: I just told ye, didn't I?! Have ye not paid a heed of a word I have said?

WENCH: Not really. I was admirin' yer pectorals.

WILLY: Well, what does any orphan rogue of a waif search high and low the world over for—journeying near and far, far and wide—driving himself half mad with grief, and the other half with rum?

WENCH: Well, it sounds like the love of a fine wench is what you're describing, if I know me obsessions. That, or a whale.

WILLY: *(bitter laugh)* Aye, a wench, you might say. But not a fine one by any means. Y'see, it was Captain Jack who left me a motherless orphan in that godless orphanage.

WENCH: You mean…?

WILLY: That's right. Captain Jack – your own Captain Jack – … is my mother.

WENCH: Your mother?

WILLY: That's right.

WENCH: Captain Jack?

WILLY: That's right.

WENCH: …is your mother?!

WILLY: Aye, you heard me the first 3 times. Captain Cecily Jack, the scourge of the seas, the captain of this vessel. The demon queen of the oceans green. She's my mother, an I'll have you know. Now will you take me to her, or do I have to keel haul it out of you?

WENCH: Stow your threats, for I'll tell you right now. *I'm* the Captain of this vessel!
> *[She grabs the cutlass out of his scabbard and takes a swing at him. He barely ducks and draws his other blade. THEY FIGHT.]*

WILLY. You! Y'are my mother? Can it be? After all these years of praying—and weeks of actually looking—I've finally found you.

WENCH. Save your wind for other sails, boy, for I am no man's mother I.

WILLY. Aye?

WENCH. Aye!

WILLY: Ye're a liar then! For the whole sea-faring world knows the legend of the dread pirate Cecily Jack, Captain of the Boatswain's Booty and how, not fifteen years agone, she took to her cabins in the midst of a storm, complaining of cramps and bloated with "sea-weight". There, she secretly gave birth to a strapping baby boy, who – fearful for her standing in the naval profession – she wrapped in an old galley cloth, and heaved him over the stern into the storm.

WENCH: Not much of a secret, then, was it?

WILLY: I stand before you today, that same strapping boy become a strapping man. An' that's the God's truth.

WENCH: Then God's a damn liar! For if your story were true, you'd barely be 15 years old.

WILLY: Aye, but a strapping 15. I mentioned I was strapping, didn't I?

WENCH: Well, I can see that for myself.

WILLY: It runs in the family. Captain Cecily Jack, it's said, was but a slip of a wee lass of 13 when she took on a whole boatload of pirates single-handed. They made her their Captain that very day, out of respect for her prowess.

WENCH: Aye, I'm full of prowess.

[She deftly disarms him and shoves her blade under his chin.]

WENCH: Now, have ye any last words before Mama tucks you in...?
To Davey Jone's locker!

WILLY: Ye'd be so callous to off your own offspring?

WENCH: For callin' me an old crone? I'd slit my own throat if I
caught me doing it.

WILLY: Yer heart is not wrenched for sorrow by the harrowsome
tale of my parentless past?

WENCH: Like ye said yourself, sailor, the whole whalin' world
knows the tale of the tot I tossed in the torrents, that stormy night,
those many years agone. And not a week goes by but you and every
other mongrel pup in Poseidon's Christendom comes lookin' for me,
claimin' to be my longlost, hopin' to snuggle a motherly hug and a
day's rate of rations out of me for pity. But the day's not half done
'fore, they're all clapped in irons and fed to the sharks, because not
one of 'em thought to mention the *golden locket* I tucked into the
seam of the wee squalling newborn's bedding - so that one day his
doting mother would know him on sight - before I dumped him off
the poop deck and into the squalls.

WILLY: I have a locket.

WENCH: Ye what?
        [She refrains from killing him.]

WILLY: Aye, a golden locket that was lodged in me gullet when
they dredged me out of the foam at New Norfolk. They had to uncork
it from me ere I could breathe right. I didn't know what it was for,
but the sisters at the orphanage let me keep it because it was too
sticky with sea goo to pawn at the rectory shop.

WENCH: Then it's true! Ye are my wee castaway bairn!

WILLY: As sure as ye're my bairn-casting mairn.

WENCH: And you've come all this way to be reunited with your prodigal mum?

WILLY: Aye, mother, I have.

WENCH: I hope yer not thinkin' we can just take up where we left off.

WILLY: Well, we left off with you heaving me to the sharks, so, no, I'd rather not start there.

WENCH: I guess that's understandable.

WILLY: Nor would I care to start any otherwhere, for I want nothing to do with you.

WENCH: What? Then why'd ye come all this way?

WILLY: To gut you like a salmon fish, ye heartless harpy!
    [He knocks her backward and seizes her weapon. THEY FIGHT.]

WILLY: I've hated you all these many years, for abandoning me when I was but a hapless swaddle, and I mean to fillet you alive for it and see if that improves me self-esteem.

WENCH: Have ye no mercy then?

WILLY: Mercy? Why, ye're lucky I don't lash you to the mainmast and flog out a drubbing for every time the cruel Sisters of Saint Salome's wore out a leather strap on my behind—*(sobs)*—when it should have been me own mum!
    [He stops fighting and starts to weep, then lunges at her – pinning her to the mast.]

WILLY: Have you naught to say for yourself, before I scuttle you like an old harbor tug?

WENCH: You'd murder your own mother?

WILLY: With no more remorse than I'd throttle a mangy wharf rat.

WENCH: Well, all right, then, do it and be quick about it.

WILLY: I'll do it when I please.

WENCH: You'll do it when I say, I haven't got all day for this.

WILLY: Don't tell me what to do.

WENCH: I'll tell you anything I like. This is still my ship.

WILLY: Ye're not the boss o' me!

WENCH: Don't sass your mother! 'Tis insubordination.

WILLY: I don't care if y'are my mother. I'll sass as I please. And I'll kill you when I kill you and not a moment before. For what you've done to me, I ought to kill my grandmother too.

WENCH: Oh, leave her be, son. The woman has cats.

WILLY: All right, my father then. I'll kill him. Where is he?

WENCH: Sweet Neptune's privy! If I knew that, you think I'd still be running a boat? It's every little girl's dream – even a successful career pirate like myself – to give up all her ambitions and raise a child in a little house with a white picket fence and a hulking man at her side to take care of her, just like in all the romance tales.

WILLY: Really?

WENCH: No, of course not.

WILLY: Then tell me who my father is. Or so help me, I'll spit you where you stand.

WENCH: You'd best go ahead and spit me then, because I haven't the slightest idea. It could be any one of these blackguards. *(She gestures toward the crew.)*

WILLY: You mean to say ye slept with your entire crew?

WENCH: Once a week, whether they needed it or not. There's not a man jack on this boat hasn't had Captain Jack's booty. Promotes morale. There's no greater loyalty than the love of a man for the only woman who'll have him. Why do you think they made me Captain?

WILLY: I thought it was because you took on a boatload of pirates single-handed.

WENCH: Aye. But I didn't use my hands.

WILLY: Ugh! You're nothing but a dirty deck harlot! A galley slattern! A cargo ho!

WENCH: Watch your mouth. I'm still your mother.

WILLY: I'd rather I were still a motherless bastard than the whoreson whelp of a scullery pump.

WENCH: It's what I had to be, son, in order to survive. The sea is a cruel mistress. And she's even crueler if you're a supple young lass on a ship full of men whose only other mistress is the cruel sea. It was either learn to love my crew, or learn to love being tied down to a galley table while my crew learned to love me. And let me tell you, they're slow learners. So I made my choices. Choices you, as a man, may never have to make.

WILLY: You forget, I was brought up in a Catholic orphanage.

WENCH: Oh, that's right.

WILLY: Why do you think they call me one-eye Willy?

WENCH: It's not because of the patch?

WILLY: No, the patch is so they don't ask me why the monks call me one-eye Willy.

WENCH: Ew.

WILLY: But we don't have to talk about that.
    [He straightens his eyepatch.]

WENCH: Am I proud of what I've done? Am I proud of tossing my only babe in a bundle off the poop deck in a storm to spare him from a life of piracy which it turns out he went ahead and took up on his own anyway? ...Frankly, no, that's kind of embarrassing. But am I proud of being able to suck a cannonball through forty feet of cast iron stove pipe? Hell, yes, I am! You try it. It's quite an accomplishment. But this is the life that chose me, son. And there's nothing for it, but to make the best chowder from what's in your net.

WILLY: I never thought of it that way. I guess I didn't know.

WENCH: There's a lot of things you didn't know about me, lad.

WILLY: But I want to know. I want us to be a family. A pirate family.

WENCH: That's all I needed to hear! Come to my arms, my brackish boy.
[They embrace. They KISS. It lasts a little too long. He suddenly pulls away.]

WILLY: Ugh! Mum! I'm your boy!

WENCH: Well, I warned you I was a fine dish of sea bass.

WILLY: You are, at that.

WENCH: I told ye.

WILLY: And how was I?

WENCH: You kiss like a shipful of sailors on shore leave.

WILLY: And that's good?

WENCH: No, that's very bad.

WILLY: Arr!

WENCH: But you'll learn...
[She puts her arm around him, and they wander off into the salty sunset...]

WILLY: So how'd you come to find yourself alone at 13 on a boat full of pirates in the first place?

WENCH: They answered my ad.

BLACKOUT

A MIDNIGHT CLEAR

I. B. HAMILTON

A Midnight Clear premiered in April 1998 at Cafe Copioh in Las Vegas, Nevada, under the title "Good Friday." The production was directed by Curtis C. The cast was as follows:

LUKE: John Lysaght
PAUL: Jake Bendel

SETTING:

A small examination cubicle in a hospital emergency room.

The play was further developed at the 9th Annual New Play Development Workshop, under the direction of Judith Royer, at the August 1998 Meeting of the Association for Theatre in Higher Education in San Antonio, Texas (made possible, in part, through a grant from the Nevada Arts Council); – and through a staged reading, produced by BrazenHeart Productions, and under the direction of Abbe Levin, at the Pulse Theatre on 42nd Street, in New York City, September, 1998.

[LUKE, in hospital gown, facing upstage. He moves gingerly, in obvious pain. PAUL enters and pauses. He wears an inexpensive, plain black suit and carries a gym bag.]

LUKE: Lay one latex finger on this body before that magic elixir of yours kicks in, and you eat mistletoe, Nurse Ratchet. *(pause)* 'Matter Ratchet? You losing your—

PAUL: Luke?

LUKE: Paul?

PAUL: I . . . they called that you were here and—

LUKE: What?

PAUL: I—I'm still listed as emergency contact on your records.

LUKE: Oh. I didn't know . . . *(turning, he reveals severe bruising on his face)* They shouldn't have—

PAUL: My G— ...what hap—?

LUKE: Yeah, well. . . I guess somebody else will have to hang the decorations at the Annual Christmas "do" — but I don't think I require Divine Intervention. *(Silence)* Sorry—about the mix up.

PAUL: It's no problem. Luke, what –?

LUKE: No, really, I'll have them update the records. I'm sorry.

PAUL: They said you needed clothes. I brought a running suit . . . It's blue . . .

LUKE: Blue's nice. Blue goes with my eyes.

PAUL: I didn't bring shoes, I figured they wouldn't fit.

LUKE: *(grinning)* No, I guess they wouldn't. *(Silence)* So . . .how's the Straight, White Way and all?

PAUL: Don't. *(beat)* What happened, Luke?

LUKE: They didn't tell you? *(pause)* Ah well, ya know how it is in the wild and woolly Westside. Ah'm just moseying along and some cowboys sidle-on-up-longside me and get all bitchy-like, hurtin' my pride – so's I gotta teach 'em a lesson.
        [LUKE giggles, falters and stumbles. PAUL rushes to help.]
Whoa there, Nelly. *(pause)* I think the shot's kicked in. It's some mighty fine ambrosia. Mighty fine.
        [His giggling threatens to take him over.]
You know how ridiculous you look in that get-up?

PAUL: Yeah, well...you'd better sit down, Pahdner.

LUKE: No! No. I'll just . . . I'm fine. Fine!
        [Supporting himself on the examination table.]
Whew. There now. You should try some of this shit, Pauley— loosen you right up.

PAUL: Uh huhn. Look, is there someone I can call for you? A ... friend . . .?

LUKE: "Friend?" Oh, hey, that's a euphemism. Right?

PAUL: Let's not do this, okay?

LUKE: As in we used to be "friends" but now you've got a new "friend" – oh, and you've got God too – so we're not "friends" anymore? How very P.C. of you, Paul.

PAUL: Should I call your folks?

LUKE: No! *(beat)* Thanks.

PAUL: You can't be alone in your condition.

LUKE: May I please have that running suit now?

PAUL: I could take you to our house, but. . . we've been. . . well—

LUKE: Hell, don't worry about me, Sweetheart. I'm sure you have better—well look at that, it's Christmas Eve! You'll have sermons to write, turkeys to give away for the big day and all. Besides— wouldn't want to get Maryjane's tits in an uproar.

PAUL: Maryanne.

LUKE: Whatever.

PAUL: She's not like that.

LUKE: Then she's a better man than I am, "Friend."

PAUL: Damn it, Luke! *(LUKE grins at the profanity.)* I didn't mean that. Look, no matter what happened between us all, I—we— Maryanne and I—still care . . .You can come to our place. It'll be fine . . . I was just concerned that . . . well, Maryanne's been a little under the weather. We—

LUKE: Uh huhn. Can you get nurse Ratchet for me? I need to call a cab.

PAUL: I'm going to be a father, Luke.
[Silence. LUKE takes the running suit and fumbles with his gown's ties.]

LUKE: A daddy. Well, well, "Joy to the World." *(pause)* 'Course, as you know, I've always favored adoption, but…. Well, well, well.

PAUL: Maryanne would want us to be there for you, in spite of everything.

LUKE: In spite of everything. *(Pause)* Well, well, well.

PAUL: You need help?

LUKE: No. I've always gotten out of my clothes just fine. Thanks.

PAUL: Yeah, well... Okay, I'll just step out there, until—

LUKE: I've got boxers on—you're safe.
> *[LUKE takes of the gown he reveals bandaged ribs and more bruises.]*

PAUL: Sweet Jesus!
> *[LUKE dresses carefully.]*

LUKE: I don't think Sweet Jesus had a thing to do with this, Preacher Paul. At least I hope he didn't.

PAUL: Why would someone..? Luke, what did you get yourself into now?

LUKE: A man's got to do what a man's got to do. Isn't that right, Pauley? Hey, you woulda been proud of old manly me.
> *[LUKE feigns a macho shadow boxing match punctuating his words.]*

Yeah? Yeah? Yeah? Yeah!
> *[He wobbles, PAUL rushes to him but is waved off. LUKE giggles then stops abruptly.]*

Get the fuck out of here. Okay?
> *[PAUL hovers a moment, gives up and leaves. Improv: Calling for nurse.]*

Pauley?
> *[LUKE attempts to finish dressing, then gives up. After a long moment, PAUL returns. LUKE quickly begins dressing again.]*

PAUL: Is it true?

LUKE: You need to go home.

PAUL: The nurse said that they think you . . .that you were . . .

LUKE: Maryjane's waiting.

PAUL: Look at me, Luke. . . .

LUKE: Please go now, Pauley. Please?

PAUL: Were you raped?

LUKE: *(pause)* I had a rough date. Okay? *(pause)* Yeah. --- So ... don't worry about the running suit, Sweetheart.   I'll buy you a nice new clean one. In blue. Of course, brown would go better with your—

PAUL: Luke ... How did..? I'm sorry. I mean ... why?

LUKE: "Why?" Why?

PAUL: I mean ... why you? Where were you, what were you doing?

LUKE: "Doing?" *(laughs)* Oh, doing. Let's see, I was walking down the street naked—holding a sign that said "Spread the joy of the season—rape a fag."

PAUL: *(pause)*   I'm sorry... that wasn't ... I'm sorry. *(pause)* Did you— Do you know him?

LUKE: You know? We decided to forgo the introductions and got right down to business.

PAUL: But how—? I don't understand. You're always so caref— Did he have a gun? There was only one. Right? ... Jesus, Luke. How many—?

LUKE: Coulda been the whole fucking rodeo for all I know. Guess the ambrosia's making me a little fuzzy on the details.

PAUL: Did you recognize any of them?

LUKE: Ah, hell, Pauley, you straight guys all look alike to me.

PAUL: Don't. *(pause)* Okay, okay, look, first we'll need to call the police.

LUKE: Yeah. I know! Why don't invite all the other cops over from the neighboring bergs for a couple of donuts and a few laughs while were at it?

PAUL: I'll go with you. They'll listen to m—

LUKE: Do you still live on this planet? My "date" had stickers all over a big yellow truck saying "I support the NRA, Philip Morris, and the local fucking police!" Oh, I forgot God. They probably support Him too. Right? *(pause)* Our world's just a bit too small here, Paul.

PAUL: I don't think our world is half as small as you make it.

LUKE: You're lucky you made the big switch before you had to experience its finiteness first hand.

PAUL: Just shut up and listen for once—!

LUKE: You know what, Paul? Take your do-gooding, sanctimonious self, go back to sweet little Maryanne, raise Gilligan, Jr., and leave me in peace.

PAUL: We just . . . we've always just wanted to help you . . . We just want to—

LUKE: You just want to pray, Preacher Paul. You just want to see me humbled before the lily white alter of your Almighty Lord; begging His Almighty mercy, and - "in spite of everything" - be forgiven and filled with the Holy Spirit of Testosterone. Glory, Glory! Upon which event, I will give up my ignorant, evil ways and swagger over to the choir—Hallelujah—grab me a buxom, blond, soprano— hopefully a female and still a virgin—and without further ado—Sing it out now!—fill her with my hitherto errant seed and commence begetting. Then, and only then, Brothers and Sisters... will I be a real man, a manly man, just like the wondrous, miraculous, hypocritical, Phenomenon of the Millennium—my former "friend"—Preacher Pauley! Glory, Glory, Hallelujah, Joy to the world, Amen!

PAUL: Fuck you, Luke!
> *[LUKE laughs, then sways. PAUL catches LUKE who strikes out. PAUL helps him gently to the examination table and cuddles him.]*
Okay . . . it's okay. Shhhh. *(pause)* Why is it that every time I get within ten feet of you, I start swearing?

LUKE: 'Cause I make you feel like a manly man. I do believe it's my calling.
> *[They share the moment and a laugh then LUKE stops in pain.]*
They hurt me, Pauley. They wouldn't stop ... they—

PAUL: I know . . . I know. Shhh.

LUKE: I wasn't careful... I shouldn't have shot off my big mou—

PAUL: Shhh. It's not your fault. Something like this isn't your. . . *(pause)* What can I do?

LUKE: Nothing. Nothing, I guess. Just . . . just . . .talk to me.
> *[PAUL nods. For a moment they relax in and old comfortable way.]*

PAUL: We'll get through this, okay? Lucas?

LUKE: Mmm?

PAUL: Why the boxers?

LUKE: Because I know you hate boxers?

PAUL: *(laughing)* Did we always fight like this?

LUKE: More or less. – Maybe less.

PAUL: Did I always lose?

LUKE: Never had a chance.
    [PAUL laughs then kisses LUKE on the head.]
Paul—I—

PAUL: Shh. It'll all turn out okay.

LUKE: Pauley –?

PAUL: You'll see. Life can turn out okay. It's not easy, but . . . I
mean, things are turning out for me now. I wasn't sure they ever
would, you know...but...
    [LUKE struggles upright and PAUL moves away.]
See, it used to be that I was always yearning for something when
we—I mean after I left the world I'd always known. It was like I was
only half-alive—only half a person—always hungry deep down
inside. No matter how good things were between us, there was
always that hunger, you know? Like I was always on the outside,
looking in, or looking back at my old world, or something.... I just
wanted... So, one day it came to me. Maybe a person can't have
everything, but he can have a choice in his life—or about his life—
whatever...and I had to really think about things—about family, and,
and about my beliefs—and about choices and about...Damnit, Luke, I
needed the world I knew best ... and I ... I ...

LUKE: ...just couldn't choose love?

PAUL: ...chose a different kind of love.

LUKE: So, now you're happy. Really happy?

PAUL: *(pause)* It's a boy, Lucas. I'm having a son.

LUKE: Yes. Well, I need to dress now. Nurse Rachet will be needing the torture chamber.

PAUL: I was thinking just the other day how I hope I'll be as good a teacher as you. No, I mean it. You taught me a lot. How to ski, how to dance, even how to laugh— but nothing more profound than how important it is that a man have courage in his convictions. *(Silence)* You ever been happy, Lucas? Really happy?

LUKE: *(softly)* Yes. – But then you made a choice.
        [Silence.]

PAUL: Yeah. Okay ... I'll just ... Let me give Maryanne a call.

LUKE: Don't bother! – I mean ... She needs her rest. I hear that securing the future of Mankind is hard work for the ladies. Just get me a cab.

PAUL: It's Christmas Eve, you need . . .

LUKE: I need to be in my own little bed, Paul. In my own little bed, in my own little room – in that little world I know best. *(pause)* Call a cab. Please?
        [PAUL struggles, then surrenders and slowly moves to exit.]
Paul?
        [PAUL pauses, but does not turn.]
Tell Maryanne...tell her… Merry Christmas … tell her … congratulations for me.
        [PAUL nods and moves closer to the exit.]
Pauley?! ... Pauley . . . I . . . I'll always . . .
        [PAUL stops again.]

PAUL: I know, Lucas. I know. *(pause)* Me too.
        [PAUL exits. LUKE watches a moment, then finally smiles.]

                            END OF PLAY

BLOODY MARY

GREG VOVOS

for Jean Marie

Bloody Mary was originally produced in Cleveland Heights, Ohio in January 1999 by Dobama Theatre's Night Kitchen as part of its *Untitled* evening of One-Acts. It was directed by Ned Gallaway; Dan Kilbane was the Night Kitchen Artistic Director. The original cast was as follows:

MARY: Lara Lyn Mielcarek
JOE: Bret Hoffman
OLD LADY: Kaila Michaels
MAN IN THE SUIT: Eric Tacuit
POLICE OFFICER: Allen Branstein

SETTING:
A city street corner in the Spring. The work day is about to commence.

NOTE: If it will make the arm transfer easier, Mary can be pantsless instead of topless. Just make the changes in the script accordingly. This will allow Mary to hide her real arm inside her shirt and the pants she is not wearing can be used as her tourniquet.

A simple way to pull off the arm transfer is to build a fake arm that is masked by the sleeve of the shirt Mary is wearing, and that can be pulled off and later stashed in the inside pocket of Joe's coat. In the production I directed, we had Joe wear a long trench coat, because it made it easier to hide his "missing" leg, and we were able to stash Mary's fake arm in the inside pocket after the transfer. Mary's fake arm was a mannequin arm inside the sleeve of her shirt which was attached to the shoulder area of the shirt by Velcro. We put fake blood on the Velcro, so once it was ripped off, the blood added to the humor.

Of course there are many ways to "pull off" this bit. That's just one.

Inquiries concerning all rights should be addressed to the author at:
gregvovos@yahoo.com

[Lights up as MARY stands on a street corner holding her stomach. She removes her hands and reveals that she is bleeding badly. The sounds of the street should be very audible: car horns, conversation, shoes stomping on the pavement, etc. She looks around for help, but finds none. Using either her shirt or pants she tries to tie a tourniquet, but is unable to do so. Frustrated audibles by the actor are welcome as she struggles with the tourniquet.]

MARY: Excuse me, Ma'am—. Sir! Sir! Little boy, would you send for some help, I'm dying—. Little Boy!! YOUNG MAN, PLEASE!!! I'VE BEEN SHOT!!!
[MARY gives up. She sinks to the ground as she is very dizzy now from the loss of blood. An OLD WOMAN passes by, notices MARY and walks on without hesitation.]
Ma'am, would you please—

OLD LADY: *(Very loudly.)* I can't hear you.

MARY: I need your help. I'm bleeding to death.

OLD LADY: How can I stop your bleeding if I can't even hear you?
[The MAN IN THE SUIT enters quickly.]

MAN IN THE SUIT: Can I help you?

MARY: Yes, thank you so much. You see I've been bleeding—

MAN IN THE SUIT: Out of my way. I gotta help this old lady across the street. I do it every day and today is no different.

MARY: But I'm bleeding to death.

MAN IN THE SUIT: Ma'am, can I help you across the street?
[OLD WOMAN hits MAN IN THE SUIT with her cane as he tries to help her cross the street. MARY seems worse off than ever now. A POLICEMAN enters.]

MARY: Oh, thank Heavens, Officer. I don't know how much longer I would've lasted if you didn't come.

POLICE OFFICER: Ma'am, I'm gonna have to ask you to move on. The sign clearly reads no loitering. And you're littering all over the place. I could arrest you for that.

MARY: I'm not littering. That's blood. I'm dying.

POLICE OFFICER: That is no excuse to be topless, Young Lady. You should be ashamed of yourself. Lucky for you, I'm not on duty yet or I'd have to arrest you.

MARY: I need your help, Officer. My taxes pay your salary.

POLICE OFFICER: They certainly do. And your taxes pay the salaries of Ambulance Drivers. So let them help you. Does anyone call an Ambulance Driver when they're being robbed?

MARY: Well, of course not, but—

POLICE OFFICER: I rest my case.
[POLICE OFFICER exits quickly. MARY seems near the end of her rope. A silence and then JOE, a man with one arm and one leg, hops on. He falls in front of MARY.]

JOE: Excuse me, sorry. Very sorry.
[JOE gets up and tries to hop away.]

MARY: Please, Sir. Would you help me—? Oh my, what happened to you?

JOE: Oh, it's nothing. Nothing really. I'm quite all right actually. Well, I...I was until the lady stole my cane, but I'll be okay. I still have my job at the shoe factory, and it's only a forty-block hop away so I count myself lucky. *[Pause.]* My goodness, Miss. What happened to you?

MARY: You mean you noticed?

JOE: Well, of course I noticed. What kind of person would I be if I didn't notice you were bleeding? It looks as though you're near death.

MARY: It feels that way.

JOE: I got an idea.

MARY: What's that?

JOE: Well, maybe I could help you. I know it's a bit unorthodox, a stranger lending a helping hand these days, but why not? Today, I woke up, put on my green sock—the one with just three holes—because I knew today was going to be extraordinary. Then when I fell down my steps and the neighbor dog just licked me instead of tinkling on me, my feelings were confirmed. So I say hell yes—excuse my language—no! hell yes it is! I will help you. What can I do for you? Would you like a slice of pie?

MARY: No. No. Thank you, but no, not at the moment. Do you know how to make a tourniquet?

JOE: Well, of course. I am a learn-ed man, you know.

MARY: Could you please take my shirt and—

JOE: My name's Joe. What's yours?

MARY: Mary, Joe.

JOE: Mary Joe? No kidding. It's like fate. It's it's like we're fated together. We have the same names—

MARY: No, no, no. It's just Mary. I was calling you by your name—

JOE: Oh, oh, of course. Right. I'm so silly. I don't know what my problem is. I just, I just want everything to be perfect with the new people I meet, I want to fall in love you see, and when you said your name was Mary Joe, well then I thought praise God, here she is, the woman of my dreams, my Aphrodite, my Mary Joe—

MARY: Joe, I don't mean to be rude, but the blood's coming very quickly and I can't help myself. I need your help.

JOE: It's my appearance. I repulse you, don't I?

MARY: No, of course not. It's just...I'm. Joe! I'm bleeding to death. I need your help.

JOE: Oh now you need my help. First I repulse you just because I'm missing a couple limbs and now you need my help. Isn't that just like a woman?

MARY: Excuse me?

JOE: I loved you, Mary. And I thought you could love me too, but now—

MARY: Joe! Either help me or don't. But right now, you're—. I don't know what you're doing, but you're not helping.

JOE: Well, I could make you a tourniquet—with your shirt there, seeing as you're not wearing it at the moment.

MARY: Yes, that would be nice. That would be very sweet.

JOE: Okay, let's do it. It's a date.

MARY: All right. It's a date. Here's the shirt.
    [MARY extends her arm and JOE takes the shirt from her. He is very careful not to touch her.]

JOE: Can you hold the one end while I ... twist?

MARY: Of course.

[JOE is struggling with the tourniquet.]

MARY: Joe?

JOE: Yeah?

MARY: Never mind.

JOE: Okay.

MARY: Joe?

JOE: Yeah?

MARY: How'd you ... you know?

JOE: How'd I what?

MARY: How'd you lose your arm and leg?

JOE: Could you hold that tighter?

MARY: Sure. If you don't wanna talk about it, I understand.

JOE: Good.

MARY: You sure look cute though, when you—
        [MARY is about to touch JOE's head and he jumps away.]

JOE: DON'T!!!

MARY: What? I'm sorry. I...I was just gonna...touch you. Don't you like to be touched?

JOE: Of course I do. I just don't think you should.

MARY: Why not?

JOE: How's the tourniquet feel?

MARY: Great. It feels really nice. Thank you.

JOE: I should probably go now.

MARY: What's wrong with you?

JOE: Nothing. I just gotta get to work. And I haven't had a piece of pie yet and I can't sell shoes unless I've eaten my pie so I better just—

MARY: A minute ago you were talking about dating and now you're leaving?

JOE: I gotta...I gotta...Sometimes, I talk too much and I don't know what I'm talking about. I must've been doing that earlier. I really should go. See? I'm talking too much right now.

MARY: It's because I tried to touch you, isn't it?

JOE: No, it's not.

MARY: You've never been touched before, have you?

JOE: Yes, I have.

MARY: No, you haven't. I'm the first girl who's ever wanted to touch you, aren't I?

JOE: That's a mean thing to say, Mary.

MARY: You're right. I'm sorry.

JOE: It's not true either. I've been touched.

MARY: Sure you have, Joe. Sure.

JOE: I have. Twice.

[JOE indicates his missing limbs and MARY understands.]

MARY: Oh, I see. And every time you've been touched...

JOE: Exactly.

MARY: And you're just missing the two limbs?

JOE: Mary?!?!?

MARY: Sorry. I'm just curious.

JOE: Well, maybe you shouldn't be so curious.

MARY: What happens if you touch someone else? Then what do you lose?

JOE: I don't know. I've never touched anyone.

MARY: My tourniquet's loosening. I think you need to tighten it.

JOE: I better not.

MARY: Do you want me to bleed to death?

JOE: Of course not. I just don't want to risk...

MARY: Risk what? It's only a limb. You already lost two.

JOE: Maybe we could get someone else to do this for you. Officer! Officer!

MARY: I already tried that. You're my only hope, Joe.

JOE: I just don't think we should take any chances. I might accidentally touch you, you'll lose a limb and then where will we be?

MARY: I'd rather be limbless than lifeless.

JOE: Right. Of course.
[JOE starts to tie the tourniquet again, but is having too much trouble, mostly because he has only one hand. He is getting frustrated.]
I told you it wouldn't work. You might as well just bleed to death.

MARY: Joseph!

JOE: I'm sorry, Mary. It's just...well, this seems to be the way it always goes for me.

MARY: Try again and don't be afraid to touch me. I'm not afraid.
[JOE indeed tries again. Things seem to be going better this time. He even goes as far as to touch her arm as he ties the tourniquet. Maybe he even goes so far as to kiss her hand. However, the second he touches her arm, it falls off.]

JOE: Oh my God. What'd I do?

MARY: My arm! My arm fell off.

JOE: Mary, I'm...I'm so sorry.

MARY: Hurry up with that, Joe. I think I'm losing too much blood now.

JOE: What about your arm?

MARY: Forget my arm.

JOE: Forget your arm!

MARY: Please, just tie the tourniquet.
[JOE tries to re-attach her arm.]

JOE: I'm sure I can just re-lodge it in here for you. My grandpa was a medic in the Big War you know. So that sort of thing must run in the family ... Oops ... I'm very sorry. I'm such a klutz—

[MARY snatches the arm away from him.]

MARY: Just tie the tourniquet, Joe.

JOE: I can't, Mary. I tried and I can't.
   [JOE begins to leave.]

MARY: Joe! You're not going to leave me here alone, are you?

JOE: Of course not. I'll find help for you.

MARY: Come here.

JOE: What?

MARY: Come here.

JOE: What are you up to?

MARY: Come here. You owe me. *[He does.]* Now. Stand still. *[He does but then starts to move around, nervously.]* Stiller. *[He does.]* Now, close your eyes.

JOE: Close my eyes!?!?!

MARY: You don't trust me. Thanks to you I've lost my arm and you don't even trust me?

JOE: Okay, okay.

MARY: Good boy.
   [MARY takes her arm and attaches it to his body where he is missing an arm. It fits perfectly.]

JOE: Mary, what are you doing to me? That feels very—

MARY: Good.

JOE: Yeah, good.

MARY: Open your eyes.
[He does and discovers his new arm.]

JOE: How'd you—

MARY: Now tie my tourniquet and save my life.

JOE: But I have your arm.

MARY: Exactly.

JOE: Mary, I can't take your arm. That's too generous. I mean, it's not even Christmas.

MARY: Yes, you can. I don't need it.

JOE: Wow! Giving me your arm. That's just about the sweetest thing anyone's ever done for me.

MARY: Hurry, Joe.
[MARY begins to lose consciousness but JOE does not notice.]

JOE: It feels great. Like it's been a part of me my entire life. It's just like your body fits me like it's always been mine. Like our bodies fit together like a jigsaw puzzle. It doesn't look too feminine, does it? Mary! Mary!
[She is not responding so JOE, with his new arm, ties the tourniquet very quickly and expertly. Even though the tourniquet is tied MARY is not responding. He thinks about giving her mouth to mouth.]

JOE: Okay, Joe, you can do this. You have to do this. After all, it is your Mary Joe. I am confident my head will not fall off if I give her mouth to mouth...maybe just my lips will, my lips and my hands, that's not so bad, right?
[The Police Officer enters.]

POLICE OFFICER: Excuse me, Son. But what do you think you're doing?

JOE: Well, nothing, Officer. I'm just trying to save this woman's—

POLICE OFFICER: Save it for the Judge. You think I don't know who you are. You're under arrest.

JOE: Under arrest? For what?

POLICE OFFICER: For the theft of this young lady's arm.

JOE: She gave it to me.

POLICE OFFICER: A likely story. Come with me.

JOE: She needs our help.

POLICE OFFICER: I'm not asking you again.
    [The OFFICER advances on JOE who punches him and knocks him out. He looks at his new arm.]

JOE: Wow! That Mary is one strong girl.
    [This time he gives her mouth to mouth fearless of the consequences that might follow. MARY comes to.]

MARY: Well, it's about time. What happened to him?

JOE: Him? Ah, nothing. He just needed a helping hand so I gave it to him.

MARY: My arm looks good on you.

JOE: Thanks. You want it back?

MARY: No.

JOE: Are you sure?

MARY: If I need it, you'll be here, right?

JOE: Right.

MARY: Then I'm sure.

JOE: Well...

MARY: Well...

JOE: Whadaya say we go and get a slice of pie now?

MARY: Sounds delicious.
[They start to leave, but Mary stops them.]
Would you care to get a drink instead?

JOE: At this hour?

MARY: Why not?

JOE: Well, I do have a weakness for Blood Marys.
[They exit as lights fade to black.]

END OF PLAY

THE WEDDING STORY

JULIANNE HOMOKAY

The Wedding Story was included in the Venus Theatre festival: "Women Behaving Badly: Suffrage on Stage" (Deborah Randall, Producer,) at the DC Arts Center, Washington, DC; August, 2002. Direction and design were by Carol Herin Jordan. The cast was as follows:

STORYTELLER: Jjana Valentiner
BRIDE: Kate Revelle
GROOM: Joshua McCarthy

SETTING:
A land where grass is always green, the sun is always shining, and fences are always white picket.

TIME:
A sunny day in sunny June, the height of the perfect wedding season. In Vermont.

Inquiries concerning all rights should be addressed to the author at:
ja.homokay@att.net

Or her agent:

Marta Praeger
Robert A. Freedman Dramatic Agency
1501 Broadway, Suite 2310
New York , NY   10036
212-840-5766

[Lights up on the STORYTELLER reading from a leather-bound volume with gilded pages.]

STORYTELLER: *(closing the volume)* The End. Good night, sleep tight, don't let the bedbugs bite. What? You want to hear another one? But it's a school night. Okay, okay, just this once. I'm such a pushover. What type of story shall we hear?
[ad lib. if the audience yells out suggestions]
How about a fairy tale for our times? A field of dreams fenced in by white picket, a story of the young man and woman we all hope to be someday? Too bad, that's what you're getting.
[The STORYTELLER opens the volume back up. Lights up on BRIDE and GROOM in traditional garb standing on top of a wedding cake.]
Once upon a time there was a young woman, pretty as a day in June.
[The BRIDE does the royal wave.]
A young man stood by her side, smart as a whip and handsome as a polo horse.
[The GROOM salutes.]
They met in high school and fell in love on a merry day in May.
[The BRIDE and GROOM whisper to each other.]
Before long, the young man dropped to his knee, pulled a diamond from his pocket, and won the young woman's hand in marriage.

BRIDE: Uh, excuse us, Mr. Storyteller?
[The STORYTELLER looks back at them, confused. The BRIDE and GROOM smile and wave. The STORYTELLER waves back.]

STORYTELLER: Moving right along. With the blessings of their compatible—

BRIDE: Mr. Storyteller!

STORYTELLER: Excuse me a moment. *(to BRIDE)* Yes, what is it?

BRIDE: We didn't exactly meet in high school.

STORYTELLER: Yes you did, it says so right here.

BRIDE: We met in a bar.

GROOM: And we dated on and off for five years while she experimented with foreigners.

STORYTELLER: How nice. Well. For our purposes, let's say you met in high school, shall we?
[back to the kids]
So. With the blessings of their compatible families, the young man and woman were to be Bride and Groom.

BRIDE: *(to GROOM)* Wait a minute. As I recall, you kept breaking it off.

GROOM: What?

BRIDE: Yeah. Then you'd want me back the minute I had a new boyfriend.

GROOM: You certainly didn't waste any time running into the arms of the first guy who had an accent.

STORYTELLER: *(to BRIDE and GROOM)* Sssssh. Let's don't argue in front of the impressionable youngsters. *(to children)* The bride soon set in on the wedding preparations.

BRIDE: *(to GROOM)* I never realized you were a racist.

GROOM: I'm not, I was fine with the fact you'd slept with black men.

BRIDE: You're assuming that "racism" automatically refers to African-Americans. Isn't that a form of racism itself?

STORYTELLER: Excuse me, ma'am, sir, firmie those bouches so I can return to the story thank you.

GROOM: By all means. Don't let anything silly like our issues get in your way.

STORYTELLER: Look, will you play along? The children will have ample opportunity to be disillusioned later, let's just have a nice bedtime story, okay? Okay.
        [to the children]
AS I WAS SAYING, the preparations. They were to be married in a beautiful church—

GROOM: *(under his breath)* Drive-thru chapel in Vegas.

STORYTELLER: —followed by an elegant reception at an old inn in Vermont.

BRIDE: *(under her breath)* Back room at the Star Dust Lounge.

STORYTELLER: The bride put Martha Stewart to shame as she had the evening designed to the last detail—

GROOM: *(to BRIDE)* Ha! That really sounds like you.

STORYTELLER: —from the linen napkins to the centerpieces of purple freesia and Italian ruscus.

BRIDE: *(to GROOM)* I think he was invited to someone else's wedding.

GROOM: And why is he assuming the bride always has the taste? Does it never occur to anyone that the groom might want to participate? I worked my way through law school as a floral designer, that's how I know freesia is all wrong for a centerpiece, except maybe as an accent flower.

BRIDE: You were a floral designer?

GROOM: You need to base your arrangement on a more substantial bloom, like a lily or an orchid.

BRIDE: Brad, is there something you want to tell me?

STORYTELLER: Actually, there is something I want to tell these youngsters so they can get to bed at a decent hour. THE STORY.

BRIDE: Well huffy huff huff.

STORYTELLER: SO, they had their flawless reception for 300 guests at a turn-of-the-century inn in Vermont—

BRIDE: You know, we're not from Vermont. We've never even been to Vermont.

STORYTELLER: —at which all had a delightful time.

GROOM: *(to BRIDE)* What do you mean is there something I want to tell you?

STORYTELLER: Immediately following the splendid reception—

BRIDE: I mean, is there something you haven't been honest with me about? With yourself about?

GROOM: Like what?

STORYTELLER: The bride, at the tender age of 24—
    [The GROOM laughs out loud.]
WHAT? WHAT'S SO FUNNY?

GROOM: She's not even close to 24.

STORYTELLER: Now just wait a minute here, Buster Brown, whose story is this?

BRIDE/GROOM: Ours.

STORYTELLER: Wrong. This is a fairy tale, I'm going for prototypes.

BRIDE: But I'm 35.

STORYTELLER: In this story, you're 24. The average American woman gets married at 24.

BRIDE: How old's that make him?

STORYTELLER: 27. Why, how old is he really?

GROOM: I'm the one that's 24.

STORYTELLER: Isn't that a little young to be getting married?

BRIDE: How come 24's okay for me but not for him?

STORYTELLER: You're the woman. You're supposed to be younger.

BRIDE: Jesus.

STORYTELLER: Now, before I was interrupted for the umpteenth time, boys and girls, I was saying that after the reception, the 24-year-old bride was whisked away in a horse-drawn carriage by her 27-year-old Prince Charming.

BRIDE: Whisked away where?

STORYTELLER: I don't know. To... the... airport.

BRIDE: Which one?

STORYTELLER: The Airport of... Vermont.

BRIDE: There's one in Burlington and one in Montpelier.

GROOM: How did you know that?

BRIDE: I majored in geography.

GROOM: You did?

BRIDE: *(to STORYTELLER)* So Mr. Fancy Pants, which one was it?

STORYTELLER: The one where you caught your flight to Hawaii for your honeymoon.

BRIDE: This whole fairy tale is completely out of hand. Anyone knows there's no flights from Vermont to Hawaii. You have to fly through Logan or LAX. Or both. And anyway, I highly doubt they'd let the horses in the terminal.

STORYTELLER: Oh, for God's sake, what's the big deal in telling the children a nice little story?

BRIDE: No one's life turns out like that. How many of those kids will live up to your version of the story? None! They can't, it's too much pressure. It's like why Catholic women are all messed up, you can't be a virgin AND be a mother. And Brad, I probably shouldn't have married you to begin with.

GROOM: Shayna, how can you say that?

BRIDE: You're probably gay.

GROOM: What?

BRIDE: Oh c'mon, how many straight male floral designers do you know?

GROOM: That's what you thought I needed to be honest about?

BRIDE: You didn't even know I majored in Geography! Listen, if we're talking averages here, most people don't get married in Vermont. They get married in their one-horse hometowns that have WalMarts and bad zoning.

STORYTELLER: What's wrong with that?

BRIDE: NOTHING. THAT'S MY POINT. MOST people do get married in their hometowns. MOST people cheat on their spouses or end up in counseling or sell everything they own to get into a lousy nursing home. Put that in your fairy tale and smoke it.

STORYTELLER: No one's smoking anything. There are children present.

BRIDE: And God forbid we tell them what life is really like.

GROOM: She's got a point there. You're opening yourself up for multiple class-action suits, Mister.

STORYTELLER: Fine. I've had it. You want the truth, the whole truth, and nothing but the truth, the whole enchilada, the proverbial hook, line, and sinker? Well far be it from me to give these little souls something to which to aspire.

BRIDE/GROOM: Do it! Do it! *(ad lib.)*

STORYTELLER: I'm warning you, it won't be pretty.

BRIDE/GROOM: We stand warned.

STORYTELLER: I'm such a pushover.
          [opens the volume back up]
Once upon a time in a trailer park not so far away, there lived a woman approaching middle age who drank a lot of bourbon, smoked a pack a day, hung out in places where they throw peanut shells on the floor—

BRIDE: All right already.

STORYTELLER: —and a young, slightly effeminate man who took it up the ass once from a fellow Eagle Scout, but since it only happened once when he was 17 and drunk on Kahlua, he still considered himself straight.

GROOM: Hey hey hey.

STORYTELLER: The woman and the man met in a bar one night where they got drunk and slept together afterwards at her place. Since the woman felt guilty about the one-night stand, she felt she needed to make a legitimate relationship out of the encounter to justify the sex, even though she really prefers black men. To stay deep in the dark closet, the man proposed to the woman, and since she's 35 and, let's face it, not getting any younger, she accepted his pathetic offer because it was a real ego boost to have snagged a hot stud eleven years younger than she, even if he does have the occasional problem getting a stiffy with her because he's really gay. Although the man offered to plan the entire wedding with his best friend Steve, the woman insisted they hire a horse-drawn carriage to drop them off at the Airport of Vermont, from which they took six connecting flights to Las Vegas to get married by an Elvis impersonator. To celebrate, they showed up at the Star Dust Lounge, at which they bought all the bar patrons cheeseballs and Budweiser. When they arrived back home in Weehawken, New Jersey, the Groom, unable to suppress his inner self for a moment longer, took up with a drag queen from SoHo, and the Bride, realizing she'd never be a mother, consoled herself with vodka and Xanax and died of a somewhat accidental overdose three years later. The Groom, now 27, took up wearing cowboy hats and chaps, and made the unfortunate mistake of traveling to Wyoming on business where he was dragged to his death behind a 4x4 by a bunch of homophobic rednecks. The drag queen wrote a show about the three of them in which he played all the parts, won a Genius Grant, and landed his own talk show on New York City cable access.
        [shuts book, exits]
I bid you good night and sweet dreams, children. The End.

BRIDE/GROOM: *(ad lib., following the STORYTELLER off)* Uh, Mr. Storyteller, wait, it's okay, you can tell the other version, etc…
        [Lights down.]

* * *

HERESY AT A CROSSROADS
(IN SOUTHERN FRANCE AT TWILIGHT WHILE AFRICA REMAINS UNDISCOVERED BY THE EUROPEANS)

DOUGLAS HILL

Heresy at a Crossroads premiered at Cafe Copioh in Las Vegas, Nevada, 1998, under the direction of Greg Vovos. The cast was as follows:

DARIUS: John Lysaght
POLO: Robbie Hill

CHARACTERS:
DARIUS: A large, happy, charismatic man in his mid-thirties.
POLO: A nineteen-year-old woman, traveling light.

SETTING:
See Title.

Inquiries concerning all rights should be addressed to the author at:
doug.hill@ccmail.nevada.edu

[Dim LIGHTS UP on DARIUS who is carefully stacking a pile of rocks. Night sounds and the occasional car can be heard in the background. DARIUS stands up, looks at his rock pile and EXITS. After a moment, POLO ENTERS. She is out of breath from running and carries a school backpack. DARIUS ENTERS in with several rocks in his hands. He surprises POLO.]

DARIUS: *(a bright smile)* Good Evening. Friend or foe?

POLO: Friend. Definitely friend.

DARIUS: Looks like a definitely tired friend. Are you okay?

POLO: Yeah. I'd better keep. . . going.

DARIUS: What's your rush?

POLO: No rush. I. . . Uh. . .

DARIUS: Where're you headed?

POLO: West. Mostly. West.

DARIUS: You running from something in the east—mostly—east?

POLO: No. Huh-unh. No, my, uh, temporal life is starting. Don't want to be late.

DARIUS: I guess not. F.Y.I.?
    [He points in the direction POLO is headed.]
Our one gendarme station is at the end of this road.

POLO: Oh.
    [Pause. No one moves.]

DARIUS: And our one gendarme usually goes home after it gets dark. Pretty soon.

POLO: *(looking up at the sky and slipping off her backpack)* Thanks.

DARIUS: Sure. Just a little detail. And you don't have to worry about me. I'm always on the side of the underdog. The little people like you and me have to stick together. We're just as important as the big guys in power. And they need to learn that. Right? Right?

POLO: Right.

DARIUS: Details and the small guys. I always try to remember that. Small things are important, might does not make right, and bigger is not always better.

POLO: Okay.
> *[DARIUS quickly pulls out a small wooden cross and erects it in the pile of rocks. He presents this shrine like a vaudeville act.]*

DARIUS: So what do you think?

POLO: *(stunned)* It looks good.

DARIUS: I know its not big or anything—it looks really small next to that church over there—
> *[POLO spins around looking for the church.]*

It's kind of dwarfed in the shadow of it, but. . . what if I do. . . THIS?!
> *[DARIUS pulls out a flashlight and points it at the cross.]*

POLO: *(barely nodding her head)* Mmm-hmm.

DARIUS: Or is it better—
> *[He moves the flashlight behind the rock pile.]*

—From behind? I know it's not huge, but bigger is not always better. And I want something that won't look too commercial.

POLO: What's. . . what's commercial about a cross and a flashlight?

DARIUS: I want this to look like something from before all the hoopla—all the lawn ornaments and trinkets—Have you seen those temporary Catholic tattoos? It's just capitalism. I want something reminiscent of the days before the papal seat went hither and yon, and the whole Constantinople fiasco. Something that looks authentic to remind people of how God used to be. That's what I want people to think when they see this: Old God.

POLO: You want to trick people.

DARIUS: Yeah. Make them remember the true nature of God. So? Does it look. . ?

POLO: It looks good. It looks real nice. Very nice. I like the—

DARIUS: Oh, I get you. You're right: It doesn't look like its been around several hundred years.
 [DARIUS picks up a rock and begins pounding on the cross.]
You're a smart young lady. Verisimilitude. That's what you're saying. Ver—Is—Sim—Ill—It—Tude! It's one of the basic principles that I keep forgetting.
 [He pulls a knife out of his pocket and begins stabbing the
 cross.]
People want to see the facts with their own eyes. They want to believe and I have to help them. And you're right. I mean, come on.
 [He pockets the knife and pulls out a small handgun.]
No one's going to believe that Jews or Moslems or the other heretics have been walking by here for a hundred years if it doesn't have—
 [He fires three shots at the cross.]
—Some distress marks, huh? So you're headed west? Spain? Portugal?

POLO: Portugal. Why did you do that?

DARIUS: And what sort of temporal life are you going to find there?

POLO: Just—It's—Practical Field Cartography. You're shooting—!

DARIUS: Wow. You really don't want to be late for your first day. What is that? Car—tah—

POLO: Are you crazy? What if someone heard you?

DARIUS: Tell me, what is cartah. . ? Is it illegal? Something to do with drugs? Is that why you're—

POLO: No. It's map making.

DARIUS: Oh. And what did you call it again?

POLO: Practical Field Cartography. I'm going to draw maps and. . . I've got to get out of here.

DARIUS: Hey! Are you a Jew?

POLO: No.

DARIUS: Would you swear on the cross?

POLO: The Book of James tells us not to swear, doesn't it?

DARIUS: *(smiling)* All right. All right. That's pretty good. Glad to see you're one of us. You had me scared for a second. I heard the Jews are pretty sneaky about drawing maps and I know they let just about anyone into Lisbon these days.

POLO: Well, I'm not going to Lisbon—I'm headed for Sa. . . Good night.

DARIUS: Wait a minute! Sagres, Portugal? Prince Henry the Navigator? That Sagres? Have you prayed about this?

POLO: Before you say anything, Prince Henry needs the smartest people he can find on his expeditions. I was Co-Valedictorian, Class of 1425, Naples South High.

DARIUS: You went to school?

POLO: And I've been unemployed for a year because I refuse to cook, sew, bake, weave, or take care of snot-nosed little children.

DARIUS: What?

POLO: But I love to travel and I'm a great cartographer. I taught myself. And Prince Henry is the only one in the world who wants to really map out the—

DARIUS: Prince Henry is the anti-Christ!

POLO: No. He's Portuguese.

DARIUS: I've heard he puts north at the top of his maps. *(Pause.)* The sun don't rise in the north, kid. Think about it.

POLO: He's using the Ptolemaic method of cartography, which gives him greater precision.

DARIUS: Wait—wait. Ptolemaic? Was he a Jew?

POLO: I don't know. Greek-Egyptian, I think.

DARIUS: Okay, Ptolemaic was pagan. You see what kind of trouble you're putting yourself into? This is crazy. This is the end of the world.

POLO: It's a great adventure and he needs smart people like me taking note—

DARIUS: He needs whores to keep his sailors happy. Don't be fooled.

POLO: Have you seen his maps? They're precise. Detailed. Sailors won't have to go by word of mouth anymore. And he's opening up new routes.

DARIUS: New routes to where?

POLO: Africa, for starters.

DARIUS: He's charting the course to hell. And you're the entertainment.

POLO: Prince Henry is a Christian. Why would he be sailing into—

DARIUS: He's a heretic leading everybody into chaos and damnation and—
   [He suddenly spreads his arms out to form a "T" .]
Let me show you something. This is the world. Have you ever seen one of these? This is a map of the world. I studied it when I was living with a priest in Avignon. Who, by the way, spoke Latin. So I'd say he knew as much as a girl from Naples, wouldn't you? All right, then. Up here, where my head is? That's the east. And my head is Eden. Do you know what Eden means?

POLO: No. . ?

DARIUS: "Delightful Place." That's what it means in Hebrew— Which was the language of God's chosen people before they converted to Christianity. But I digress. "Delightful Place." And it's in the east. At the top. Where it belongs. My chest? That's Asia. The right arm is the Danube and the left arm is the Nile. My stomach, of course, is the Mediterranean Sea. Now, are you looking at this? Memorize it. Because that is the world. Does it look complicated to you?

POLO: No, but it doesn't look accurate either.

DARIUS: Okay, let's take a little test. Are you ready? Quick!— Where's Eden?—Where's Eden?—Find Eden! Come on!

POLO: There's a lot of speculation that Eden doesn't actually exist.

DARIUS: I deduct points for heresy! Now, come on! Find Eden!

POLO: *(sighs and points to his head)* Up there.

DARIUS: Up where? Don't just point to it—Touch it! You pointing
to my shoulder or neck—?
> *[POLO puts her hand on DARIUS' forehead. DARIUS bobs*
> *his head around in excitement.]*
Excellent!—That's great!—Eden! Right there at the top!—Okay!
Where's Asia? Huh? Where is it? Go find it!
> *[POLO thumps DARIUS on the chest.]*
Ding-ding-ding! Big old Asia! Right there in the center!
> *[DARIUS begins thumping himself on the chest.]*
Sounds like Mongolian drums, doesn't it? Out there in wild Asia?
DEVIL'S GONNA GET YOU KAHN! Okay! Where's the Danube
River?
> *[POLO grabs his right arm.]*
And the Nile?
> *[POLO grabs his left arm.]*
And the Mediterranean?
> *[POLO pokes him in the stomach.]*
All right! Perfect score! Five out of five! You see how easy that is?
Now why would a loving God want to take something so simple and
make it hard? It's been a perfect model for years.

POLO: But Prince Henry's method isn't hard. All you do is—

DARIUS: Okay, let's try it from Prince of Darkness, Henry's point of
view.

POLO: Everything just rotates around.

DARIUS: All right. What's my right arm?

POLO: Well, your right arm would become the, uh, the
Mediterranean.

DARIUS: Mmm-hmm. And my head?

POLO: Your head is the Danube.

DARIUS: My head is what?

POLO: The Danube River.

DARIUS: That's the top of the world? Oh brother. And what does "Danube" mean in Hebrew?

POLO: I don't know.

DARIUS: Well, it's probably not "Delightful Place" huh? Okay, what's on the left?

POLO: Um. Eden—if it exists—would be over there—

DARIUS: Eden is on my left? How can Eden—? Do you know what I do with my left hand? Wait a second. I'm lost, now. Where did you say Asia was?

POLO: Oh—uh, well—

DARIUS: Okay, skip it. Can you find Africa and the Nile at least?

POLO: That'd be your stomach.

DARIUS: So you want to draw maps of my belly? Does that sound smart to you? Does that sound like something a Co-Latin graduate would do?

POLO: Well, you're not an exact map of the world. That's the point. And Prince Henry's already mapped most of northern Africa. He's sending expeditions further south.

DARIUS: *(looking at his waist)* You want to explore that?

POLO: Look. . .

DARIUS: Doesn't that scare you a little?

POLO: We're not going to be exploring your. . . your, uh. . .

DARIUS: Touch it if you aren't scared of it, then.

POLO: The point we're making is more figurative than literal.

DARIUS: Go on. You're not scared. Touch it. Like you did Eden.

POLO: Uh, uh, no. I mean, no.

DARIUS: *(pointing his gun at POLO)* Come on, friend. You're one brave cartwheeler, aren't you? Go ahead and touch the uncharted regions of Africa like Prince Henry wants you to. Touch that vile den of carnal knowledge. Some call it the doorway to Hell itself.
[DARIUS unbuckles his belt.]
But you're not scared. You want to go there because Prince Henry tells you its okay. Remember? You want to go and draw maps of deepest darkest Africa. Look at it.
[As DARIUS opens his fly, POLO quickly picks up the cross and holds it between them.]

POLO: Please don't. I'm unarmed. I don't want to invade your— please don't shoot me.

DARIUS: Well, of course I wasn't going to shoot you. But you see? Your heart is telling you what Prince Henry's doing is wrong. Look at you. You're clinging to a cross facing the barrel of a loaded gun, because deep inside you know the difference between right and wrong. And I figured you did, being a Christian and all. So be afraid. You're not a whore. You're smart. Go back to Naples and fear the devil and all his works. Fear the power he has over the weak in mankind. And the Lord will reward you forever.

POLO: But I can't do practical field cartography there! No one believes in it!

DARIUS: Then do something else. It's only your temporal life. Look at me.

POLO: I can't put up shrines for the rest of my life!

DARIUS: This? This isn't my job—This is penance. I can't make a living doing this. No, I'm a district manager for a chain of childcare centers: "Suffer the Little Children." We've got five centers in France and I'm—

POLO: I'm not going to baby-sit either! I'm going to work for Prince Henry! He's the only one who believes like I do. In the precise, detailed truth. The rest of you can hang on to your myths about Eden, and your fairy tales and lies and . . . and I don't care if it comes straight out of the pope's mouth, it's still a lie—

DARIUS: *(grabbing the cross from her)* I thought you were on our side.

POLO: I can't do anything else. I have to make maps. I have to tell the truth.

DARIUS: Friend or foe? Friend or foe?
    [He bludgeons POLO with the cross. She falls and he towers over her, ready to strike again.]
Friend or foe?

POLO: Friend. Definitely friend.

DARIUS: *(smiles brightly and extends a hand to help her up)* All right, then. You heretics sure are a handful, aren't you?
    [POLO starts to get up, kicks DARIUS in the groin and scurries away as he sinks to his knees.]

POLO: It's not heresy.

DARIUS: Ohh, my God. . .

POLO: You're all wrong! It's not heresy! Stop chasing me!
    [POLO EXITS quickly. DARIUS remains on the ground.]

DARIUS: I should have seen it coming. . .

BLACKOUT

CARMEN DICK:
Feminist Private Eye

BRIAN E. ROCHLIN

Carmen Dick: Feminist Private Eye premiered on September 10, 2005, as part of "Day Players" at the ACME Comedy Theatre in Los Angeles, California, under the direction of Brian Wittle. Producers were Jenelle Riley, Sondra Mayer, and Anthony Backman. The cast was as follows:

CARMEN DICK: Tenaya Cleveland
ARMENEH HABIB: Mikhail Blokh
BRUCE VAGINA: Patrick Thompson
HORNY CARMELLA: Jules Bruff

CHARACTERS:

CARMEN DICK, Feminist Private Eye: She's hard-boiled. A gumshoe of the first order, always in control. She barely hides a raging, dominant sexual beast.

ARMENEH HABIB: Male (although he was named after his maternal grandmother). Middle Eastern...or is he Armenian? No really, where is that accent from? Proprietor of the Marvelo Magic Shop/Beer Garden. He believes that all other magicians are hacks!

BRUCE VAGINA: (pronounced Vaj-in-Ay) A bit of a male chauvinist pig. He doesn't like to be told what to do, but hasn't had sex in sooooo long, he would willingly don a leather mask and diaper if there was the promise of getting laid. He wants to be the world's greatest magician, and hopes to learn everything he can from Habib.

HORNY CARMELLA: Bisexual monogamist, but only she knows it (the monogamist part, that is). She is very accommodating. Doesn't want to rock the boat. Habib is her ex-boyfriend. She had a one-night stand with Carmen, but both try to conceal it.

SETTING:
A rain-slick street. A noir-ish magic shop/beer garden

TIME:
Yesterday

NOTES: There is a warped reality to this world. Props are never completely normal. They are either imaginary or somehow blown out of proportion.

Carmen's linguistic style is stylized; straight out of 40s detective noir films. Characters can seem like they come from different realities.

Inquiries concerning all rights should be addressed to the author at: BRochlin@aol.com

EXT. STREET CORNER

[The sound of rain and thunder behind dramatic private eye music. Carmen Dick, a woman wearing a trench coat and fedora, stands alone in a SPOTLIGHT.]

CARMEN DICK: It was a dark and stormy night.
[LIGHTS OUT/MUSIC STOPS/RAIN CONTINUES.]
I mean it was twilight. Just post storm.
[RAIN ENDS/SPOTLIGHT UP.]
The streets were wetter than my pants after 12 hours of watching gladiator films. Danger was in the air, and I was on a case. My name is Carmen Dick: Feminist Private Eye.

INT. MARVELO MAGIC SHOP AND BEER GARDEN

[LIGHTS UP on the shop. ARMENEH HABIB (proprietor), BRUCE VAGINA (customer), and HORNY CARMELLA (customer), sit around a table. Bruce drinks from a huge cardboard bottle of beer.]

ARMENEH HABIB: That David Copperfield is nothing but a hack, a dickless hack.

HORNY CARMELLA: I don't know. I saw him make an entire airplane disappear. Well, I didn't actually see it, because, you know, it disappeared. But it was magical. He's very cute.

ARMENEH HABIB: Hack. David Blaine...Hack! Ricky Jay...Hack! Penn and Teller...Hacks! Doug Henning...

BRUCE VAGINA: Dead Hack!

ARMENEH HABIB: That is damn right!

CARMEN DICK: I entered the Marvelo Magic Shop and Beer Garden. It stunk of stale Pilsners and stale lives.
[She enters. Armeneh gets up.]

107

ARMENEH HABIB: We are closed for the twilight. I am so sorry.

CARMEN DICK: No. You're not. But you will be. Mark my words.

HORNY CARMELLA: Hi. Who are you?

CARMEN DICK: I'm Carmen Dick: Feminist Private Eye.
[She rolls the fedora off her head, down her arm, catches it, and places it on the table.]

BRUCE VAGINA: Yeah, well I'm Bruce Vagina: Chauvinist Private Citizen.

CARMEN DICK: Vagina. Would you mind spelling that?

BRUCE VAGINA: Yes. Yes, I would.

HORNY CARMELLA: *(sidling up to her)* You're a detective. That's very sexy.

CARMEN DICK: *(aside)* She had legs that went all the way up to her firm, delicious, and very penetrable, buttocks.

HORNY CARMELLA: Thanks. So do you.

BRUCE VAGINA: So do I.

CARMEN DICK: *(to Armeneh)* And who might you be?

ARMENEH HABIB: I am Armeneh Habib, proprietor, and that is Horny Carmella, my bisexual ex-girlfriend. What are you doing here?

CARMEN DICK: I'm here to investigate a murder.

BRUCE VAGINA: There's no one dead here.
[Carmen pulls out a gun (actually her two fingers pretending to be a gun) and shoots Armeneh, who falls to the ground.]

CARMEN DICK: Says you.

BRUCE VAGINA: You crazy bitch!

CARMEN DICK: You really are a chauvinist, Mr. Bruce (pronounced as it's spelled) Vagina.

HORNY CARMELLA: You know, I always wanted to be a detective. Perhaps I can help.

BRUCE VAGINA: You shot him!

CARMEN DICK: Did I? *(aside)* I knew this Bruce (prounounced as it's spelled) Vagina would be no help. He had the look of a man who'd been anally penetrated three too many times.

BRUCE VAGINA: You know we can hear you?

CARMEN DICK: *(aside)* Could they truly hear me?

HORNY CARMELLA: Yeah, we can.

CARMEN DICK (V.O.): Then perhaps I should talk in voice over.

HORNY CARMELLA: I really want to help with the investigation.

CARMEN DICK (V.O.): I like talking in voice over. I sound sexy.

BRUCE VAGINA: We know who did it!

CARMEN DICK: Or do we? The first rule of detection is never jump to conclusions.
    [Armeneh sits up.]

ARMENEH HABIB: *(aside)* For example, they don't know it, but I'm not dead yet.
    [He lies back down.]

CARMEN DICK (V.O.): For example, I don't know it, but he's not dead yet.

BRUCE VAGINA: I'm calling the police.

CARMEN DICK: *(pulling out her gun)* Not so quick.
   [Bruce lifts his cardboard beer bottle, defensively.]

ARMENEH HABIB: *(aside)* I'm actually feeling pretty good...except for the agonizing pain of this gunshot wound.

CARMEN DICK: As a feminist detective, I can tell you that your huge beer bottle is a feeble attempt to compensate for a small and ineffectual penis.

HORNY CARMELLA: I could have told you that.

ARMENEH HABIB: *(aside)* Did she sleep with Vagina, too? If it weren't for the massive blood loss, I'd confront her right now.

BRUCE VAGINA: I've had enough of you.
   [He SMASHES the cardboard bottle. We hear the bottle break.]

CARMEN DICK: No you haven't.
   [She removes her trench coat, and throws it to the floor, where it makes the same SMASHING sound as the bottle. She is wearing only a bra.]

BRUCE VAGINA: I want to explore the deep, depraved cavities of your mind.

CARMEN DICK: *(aside)* It wasn't my mind he wanted to explore.

HORNY CARMELLA: I thought you were a feminist.

CARMEN DICK: I'm a contemporary feminist. *(to Bruce)* Come here.

[They begin making out, Bruce still holds on to the bottle.]

BRUCE VAGINA: I love you.

CARMEN DICK (V.O.): He had all the technique of epileptic eel, but he loved the taste of my larynx.

HORNY CARMELLA: You never kissed me like that.

ARMENEH HABIB: *(aside)* I was right. Oh, I'm really in a caravan of pain now.

CARMEN DICK: Do you really love me?

BRUCE VAGINA: I do.

CARMEN DICK: Would you do anything for me?

BRUCE VAGINA: Yes, anything.

CARMEN DICK: Would you kill for me?

BRUCE VAGINA: I would kill for you.

CARMEN DICK: Would you die for me?

BRUCE VAGINA: I would die for you.
[She has taken hold of the beer bottle, and stabs him in the back. He grimaces in pain and falls to the ground.]

CARMEN DICK: *(casually)* Thanks.
[She picks up the bottle, takes a swig and puts it on the table. Horny is finally horrified.]

BRUCE VAGINA: *(from the floor, unmoving)* You killed me.

CARMEN DICK: Did I? Horny, I think we should continue our investigation.

HORNY CARMELLA: I'm not... I don't... There's nothing to investigate. You killed them both.

CARMEN DICK: Do you really believe that?

HORNY CARMELLA: What do you mean? Of course I believe that. I can't believe I was ever attracted to you.

CARMEN DICK: I mean, do you really think I killed Habib and (pronouncing it as it's spelled) Bruce Vagina?

BRUCE VAGINA: It's Vag-In-Ay!

HORNY CARMELLA: I saw it. Both times, I saw it.

CARMEN DICK: Did you? Or did you see the work of a master illusionist? A master illusionist by the name of Armeneh Habib.

HORNY CARMELLA: He couldn't have killed himself and Bruce Vagina. He's dead.

CARMEN DICK: Perhaps you're mistaken. Perhaps he's not dead.
    [Habib struggles to his feet. He is clearly in tremendous pain.]

ARMENEH HABIB: Perhaps I'm not.

HORNY CARMELLA: *(to CARMEN)* I don't care if he's not dead. *(to HABIB)* I mean, yes, I care. We did date. *(to CARMEN)* But he couldn't have killed them. I saw you kill them both.

CARMEN DICK: You couldn't have seen me. You couldn't have seen me kill them because I don't really exist.

ARMENEH HABIB: It's true.

CARMEN DICK: Armeneh Habib is a master illusionist. All the others... hacks!

ARMENEH HABIB: Hacks!

CARMEN DICK: He created me, his master illusion. After six months, two weeks, and 4 days of dating him, you should have known how good he is. Besides, after all, there's no such thing as a feminist detective. Sure, there are those who would say Gloria Steinem and Simone du Beauvoir were detectives into the world of gender relations, defining a heretofore undefined feminism, but that's not what we're talking about here.

ARMENEH HABIB: It really isn't.

HORNY CARMELLA: I don't understand.

CARMEN DICK: After you broke up with Habib, he was devastated. Night after night, he would daydream of getting you back.

ARMENEH HABIB: Night after lonely night.
    [He falters.]

HORNY CARMELLA: Are you all right? I thought all this was an illusion.

CARMEN DICK: No, the gun was real. He's a great illusionist, but a lousy shot.

ARMENEH HABIB: It is true. Oh, the pain is most great.

HORNY CARMELLA: I don't see any blood.

CARMEN DICK: Exactly. A great illusionist. First he pretended to kill himself, hoping you would want to find out who did it. But really, he wanted to discover whether you were having an affair with Bruce, as he had suspected for months.

HORNY CARMELLA: But I wasn't. The only person I'd been with since Habib was you.

CARMEN DICK: And you were quite good.

HORNY CARMELLA: Thanks.

CARMEN DICK: How was I?

HORNY CARMELLA: Eh. *(Trying to figure it out)* But wait, if you don't really exist, how could I have sexually devastated you?

CARMEN DICK: You weren't that good.

ARMENEH HABIB: I would also daydream about you being with another woman.
   [He groans in pain.]
That's really an awful lot of blood.

CARMEN DICK: Yes, our time together was merely a product of Habib's daydreams. A lesbian fantasy brought to life.

HORNY CARMELLA: But it was my daydream.

CARMEN DICK: He's that good! When I was making out with Bruce, and you said, "You never kissed me like that," Habib's worst suspicions were confirmed. And so he killed Bruce.

ARMENEH HABIB: Could you call an ambulance, please. I believe I am dying.

HORNY CARMELLA: Wait a minute. If he concocted our tet-a-tet, wouldn't he have known I meant YOU never kissed me like that.

ARMENEH HABIB: Ow. Ow. Ow.

CARMEN DICK: He's a great illusionist, but not very smart. No man is when he is consumed by jealousy.

HORNY CARMELLA: His jealousy... *(to HABIB)* Your jealousy. That's why I broke up with you in first place.

ARMENEH HABIB: Why didn't you just say so. I can change. I really can... I feel so very cold. Mother?

CARMEN DICK: Yes, no man is smart when consumed with jealousy. Few are smart to begin with. I should know. I'm Carmen Dick: Feminist Private Eye.
> *[Simultaneously Armeneh and Carmen collapse. Horny picks up the trench coat and puts it on. She flips on the fedora. A spotlight shines on her.]*

HORNY CARMELLA: Not any more. Now I'm Carmen Dick: Feminist Private Eye.

ARMENEH HABIB: *(from the ground)* You killed me.

HORNY CARMELLA: Did I?

                    LIGHTS OUT

THE WEED DREAMS

ERIC KAISER

Inspired by a true story from *The Gulag Archipelago* by Aleksandr Solzhenitsyn

The Weed Dreams was originally produced in 1999 by Poor Playwrights Theatre, Las Vegas, Nevada, under the direction of Laura Rin. The cast was as follows:

X: Linsey Hamilton
Y: Jamie Carvelli
Z: Ernie Curcio

CHARACTERS:

X.: X should be older than Y. or Z. X. has been a part of this system for so long that she comes across almost robotic, however, she is totally adept to her environment. Her Lucidity comes across in waves. She almost always looks forward at the leader's podium.

Y.: Y. should be younger than X. but older than Z. Y. isn't as robotic as X. Y. is in that middle ground, more paranoid and a more malicious than X. Y's lucidity is more of a consistent, however her paranoia takes almost all of her brain space.

Z.: Z. is the youngest. This is his first day. He is fresh and completely human. He is so excited that he is almost reckless in his enthusiasm for the system.

POSSIBLY TWO GUARDS: They should all be wearing some sort of official looking uniform, whatever it looks like they should all be wearing the exact same.

SETTING:

We should feel that we are looking at a packed room. The stage should be filled with chairs and the actors can act like all of those chairs are full. The audience is presumably the Leader's podium.

The air is very tense. Any wrong thing said or done could result in immediate death or imprisonment, and everyone knows it. However, everyone also knows that the more nervous you are the more you are scrutinized by those higher than you. So all the actors try and act as calm and as happy as possible.

Inquiries concerning all rights should be addressed to the author at: vladigogo@hotmail.com

[X. is the first to enter, she must act like all the chairs are full except for the three she is walking to, she calmly apologizes to all the people as she gets to her chair.]

X.: Slightly Sorry. Slightly sorry. Slightly Sorry I'm almost late. Good to see you. Slightly sorry I'm almost late.
[The second X. sits, Y. enters. Y. does not hide her nervousness as well.]

Y.: *[Also talking to the imaginary people.]* Sorta Sorry, sorta sorry, sorta sorta sorry. How are you? You're not mad, I'm almost late. Sorta Sorry. Sorta Sorry.
[Y. sits next to X.]

X.: *[Suddenly very authoritative.]* You're late.

Y.: Almost late.

X.: Almost late is late.

Y.: Only almost.

X.: You think the leader would agree? The new leader? Agree that being five minutes early is early? That's late. You're late. Late. God forbid he finds out.

Y.: When did you get here?

X.: Been here.

Y.: Since when?

X.: Since before you when, and that's early enough.

Y.: 'Early enough?' Sounds more like duty than honor and privilege. I was spending time getting extra special ready, like a political consummation. A prepubescent coital dream of excitement at the leader, that's why I wasn't as early as could have been.

119

X.: He doesn't care about such details, just the facts. And the fact was you're late.

Y.: So now you're assuming what he thinks? What do we need him for if you have already decided his thought? You can do better than him?

X.: *[Not knowing how to rebut.]* You should have been earlier, and if it comes down to it, I won't hesitate to say what I saw.

Y.: And what did you see?

X.: You know what I saw, I saw you being late. And if I need tell the leader I will you canker sore.
> *[She sees Z. walking in. Z. takes a while to find an opening in all of the seats.]*

It is alright. Alright. He is later than we. Alright. *[Pause.]* I'm getting too old for this...Sweet leader forgive. Nice to see you again. Your life is good?

Y.: I am Alive, my children are alive...all is good thanks to the leader. You're children are alive?

X.: *[Pause. As a wave of lucidity hits her.]* I, Getting old, getting tired. Want sleep...want dream...my young girls dreams were dreamt...and came true...dreamt wrong want dream again. Getting old, and cold. Need new dreams. Mine and theirs. All the good I dreamt turned not good. All we did and do to help, only helped a few, a few that did not need the help, Young green leaves forced to brown crushed in the street for new shiny shoes to hear the crunch, the love of the crunch.

Y.: *[Y. is in shock that those words were said. She is terrified she might be associated with them.]* I'm sorry I didn't hear you. Too busy waiting for the leader. Too excited for more glorious changes and ideas. I did not hear you. I did not hear her.

X.: Lotta young ended for the true and good. Lotta young. No longer matter no more, upstairs going take from me soon, all I have left to take, let them have it. Force of habit my love of this.

> *[Z. is unapologetic about his lateness, he just walks over to X. and Y. Z. sits. X. instantly reverts to her prior systematic self.]*

Z.: Wow, huh? Wow. My first time here. How exciting. Huh?

X.: You are late.

Y.: Very late.

Z.: It's one minute till.

X.: That is late.

Y.: Very late.

Z.: *[Confused.]* But…I'm early.

X.: One minute?

Y.: That counts as early now?

X.: He, you think *he*—

Z.: Who?

X.: Who?

Y.: Who?

X.: Him. The leader, the new glorious leader. He will tolerate tardiness.

Z.: But—

Y.: Last one here. That's later than everyone else. We've been here.

X.: Long time now.

Y.: Couldn't wait to see him. Been here all day.

X.: I here all day also.

Y.: Her too.

Z.: Well...am I in trouble?

X.: Lotta people always in a lotta trouble.

Y.: 'Course not us, we love the leader.

X.: Love him.

Z.: Well, so do I.

X.: Didn't love him enough to get here early.
[Suddenly all three see the leader, they stand up and start clapping, a tape of huge applause can accompany the three. The three will continue clapping until the end of the play. Even though after a few minutes their hands will hurt, they still try and smile as large as they can. If the sound of their clapping is too obtrusive, they can silently clap.]
The leader. I love the leader.

Y.: I love the leader.

Z.: We love the leader.

X.: No, no, no we. Only I truly love the leader and I will show it to him.

Y.: I love him more.

X.: Not more than I.

Y.: Much more.

X.: Yeah. I'm an old Woman, I loved him longer.

Y.: But he's new to all of us.

X.: I'm older. I've seen lotsa leaders. Lotsa leaders. None like him.

Y.: You've never seen him.

X.: Stop ruining his moment. This is his moment not ours. Your clapping is a shoddy mess. Clap like you mean it.
[The three continue to clap, their faces contort a bit in pain, still all three all smiles.]

Z.: *[Whispering.]* When can we stop?

Y.: *[Jumping at the opportunity.]* When you want child. Whenever you want.

Z.: Why is no one else stopping?

Y.: Waiting for you to stop first child. You're the youngest, no children to lose.

Z.: No children yet. Soon. Very Soon.

X.: Very soon.

Z.: And to think that my children will soon prosper and dream under the love and truth of the leader. A new healthy crop grown under the leader's new compassionate and fair sun. Where there are no weeds, only green fertile life. And I will fight my life to harvest that crop. I dream of that green fertile land. Green fresh life…my hands hurt.

Y.: Then stop!

X.: Give the child a chance! Keep clapping…why do you love the leader?

Z.: Well…

X.: Faster.

Z.: Clap?

X.: Answer. Why you love the leader? Why? Love the leader, why?

Z.: Well—

X.: No 'Well' only why. Now!!

Z.: Because…he…he…

X.: You want your kids? Wanna see 'em? Why you love the leader?

Z.: My hands hurt.

Y.: They should let them hurt, all the leader will give to you and you can't stand a little hand heat?

X.: Stop. Why you love the leader?

Z.: Well—

X.: No 'Well.' You love him because he is a god on earth, with the foresight and compassion of the divine. The leader is the gardener, we his hoe. We have no idea the weeds from the crop. We are a blind tool without his sight…and so on. Keep clapping.

Z.: My hands hurt.
   [The clapping gets more frantic, the pain is visible on their faces, they still try and smile. The lines overlap, the heat and pain in their hands manifest in their fast and furious talk. These lines can overlap.]

Y.: Well then stop.

X.: Don't stop.

Y.: We never whined like this. Makes me sick. A weed, he's a weed. I'm a crop. He a weed.

X.: We all weeds.

Z.: This is crazy.

X.: Don't stop clapping.

Z.: Someone's gotta stop.

X.: Not you child. Your dreams still time for dreamt.

Y.: Why you care?

X.: Let me care. Don't stop child.

Y.: We do this for a reason. Weed out the weeds.

X.: Don't listen to him child. Keep clapping. Be a crop.

Z.: My hands hurt.

Y.: Whiney weed.

X.: Shut up.

Y.: Why you care?

X.: Don't matter.

Y.: Why you care?

X.: Let me care.

Z.: My hands hurt.

X.: Keep clapping.

Y.: You stupid old canker, why you care.

X.: Let there be one green leaf.

Z.: AAAAAAAAAAAAAAAAAAAAAAAAAHHHHHHHHHHHHH
HHHHH!!!!!!!
*[And with the scream, Z. stops for a millisecond. All of the
audience, X. And Y. included, take his initiative, and also stop
clapping, they sit. It must be clear that Z. Stopped first.]*

Y.: Goodbye kid.

Z.: What?
[Two Burly guards with guns rush in, and grab Z.]

Y.: The leader has no time for the lazy and the weak. The weeds.
[They begin to drag Z. off-stage. X. Stands up.]

X.: It was me!!! I stopped first, not him…you saw the wrong one.

Y.: What are you doing?

X.: I did it. I did it, not the child. I don't have the time to waste on
(referring to the leader) him. No more time to waste on him. It was
me. I am a weed. I have dreamt of a poison crop for my children.
*[The guards drop Z. and rush to X. They pick her up and drag
her off.]*
DREAM YOUR NEW DREAMS child. DREAM NEW
DREAMS!!!!!!!!!!!!!!
[X. is gone. Z. sits next to Y.]

Z.: Where's she going?

Y.: Out with the other weeds. Just shut up and listen.

[There are two possible endings. You choose.]

[A: Over the loudspeaker the leader says one word, then suddenly in the wings of the stage, death screams drown out the leader. The lights fade on Y. Then Z.]

[B: Over the loudspeaker the leader says one word, then suddenly Y. and Z. stand up again and clap. Like before as lights fade.]

END OF PLAY

Printed in the United States
207034BV00003B/148/A

9 781430 300229